Scorched Earth
Volume I

A Percentile RPG Story

Ethan Moore

Cover art by Kaitlyn Combs

ISBN: 978-1-968612-12-2

Printed in the U.S.A.

Contents

Chapter One
September 23rd, 2114
College Station, Texas
Gertrude Alvarez

A long green sign hung from an old intersection. It had white letters on it that spelled 'T.E.X.A.S A.V.E.' Gerti couldn't read what it said, but it swayed back and forth in the storm-darkened wind. She had never learned to read properly. She recognized the English alphabet but they all just looked like glyphs to her. Gerti understood they could be put together to make words but it never really helped with her job before so she never bothered to learn.

It was against the Council's laws for outer wall citizens to read - that right was reserved for the council's upperclassmen. Less than a handful of other outerwall citizens were allowed the exclusive privilege. Her dad and the pastor. The council had tried to crack down on

4

the pastor but the people took up arms - so the council backed off.

Her employers gave her instructions to look for an item with certain symbols on them and that's what she would do.

Gerti was still waiting for the sun to rise just a little further before she continued her search. She knew the 'Trustee Bots' could see in darkness and she didn't want to give them an advantage - if she could help it. She had traveled ninety miles south through the scorched and arid lands of Texas. She'd be damned if she died this close to what she was looking for.

The building she had hunkered down in was an old diner that had fallen apart with time. The walls were scorched from the Rebirthing fires and the windows were blown inward. Shattered glass and sandy mud filled every crevice of the diner. The wind rustled down the street and filled the diner with the smell of rain. Small droplets began falling in through the open roof.

Rain had become a very rare thing but Texas still had hurricanes rolling in from the gulf every year so reliably you could set your watch to it. The rain droplets were followed shortly by a heavier shower that caused Gerti to grab her rifle and bag before retreating behind the dusty old counter.

Her rifle was old and prone to rusting. It was a larger caliber, bolt action rifle with a wooden stock and iron sights - Gerti only used it for dire circumstances.

After a few minutes of rain, she wrapped her rifle in a long oilcloth and tucked it under her arm. The rain was a nuisance, but she needed to get a move on and she knew the bots wouldn't be able to operate as well in the rain. She pulled her dirty black hair from her face and stuffed it under a baseball cap. It did little to keep her dry.

She was wearing a baseball shirt with long green sleeves and a gold collar that matched her hat. There was the face of a black bear printed on the gray front. It was the sigil of the council that hired her.

She made her way to "The University" as the council had called it. They treated it with an air of reverence that surprised Gerti - they were also based out of the carcass of a crumbling university. She weaved between what was left of the town towards the school through dilapidated and burned houses - many of which had completely collapsed. She went slow and easy like her mother had taught her - silent as a ghost. Each shadow and movement were suspect to scrutiny. Each loose framing board swinging in the wind was a possible bandit, mutant, or bot.

She came to a wide road with a row of old burnt out businesses along it. Across the road she could see the university. Massive brick structures filled the skyline across an imposingly open field of rain soaked ground.

She scrunched her nose at a foul smell. She followed the scent to a large creature that had crawled up next to a crumbling house before dying - several days ago by the smell. Gerti threw a rock at it and crouched behind a burnt out car. It didn't move. She looked around and quickly ran towards the corpse. It was severely rotted but Gerti excitedly looked until she found what she was looking for.

Tiny crimson beads were suspended in its black fur. She plucked a few out - exposing a patch of blood that hadn't completely dried. She watched the dark blood slowly form into the valuable crystals. She grabbed those and turned the creature over - it had the face of a man. She didn't flinch. She was used to seeing these horrors.

Gerti's mother had taught her most of what she knew about the wasteland: *"Don't whistle when you're out there - you don't know what you'll attract,"* was one bit of advice that always sent shivers down her spine. Her mother had never specified what the whistling attracted and Gerti never asked. The wind and rain howled through the dead city. *"Don't take the bait,"* was another piece of sage motherly advice.

She got low and looked at her surroundings. There was an apartment and a large brick building with gaping jagged glass windows nearby. She examined the windows until she was more or less satisfied she wasn't sitting in an unsprung trap.

Her attention returned to the mutant but she moved faster. A deep circular wound surrounded in black charred skin and singed fur filled its torso. The

7

inside of the fleshy crater was plastered with crimson crystals. She hastily chipped off as much as she could before stuffing them in a small bag she carried. She estimated there was, at least, a pound of crystal - maybe fifteen in total. That would be a hefty bonus to this job.

She left the dead mutant and carefully entered one of the burned out businesses facing the school. It had been some sort of cafe. Leather seated booths were torn, cracked, and faded from the endless onslaught of the oppressive sun.

She removed her rifle from its bag and slowly cleared the building, trying to make as little noise as possible. She eventually felt secure in the idea she was alone. She settled into a cracked booth and watched the field for any details that would help her.

On the other side of the field to the left, there was a truly massive square building with the insignia of the old university. Gerti recognized the symbol from her travels. There was an old wooden barn with it scrawled on the roof - it had collapsed but the letters were still legible. Gerti assumed this university must have been some kind of cult from before the fires.

She had seen their symbol on clothes, old cars, houses, furniture, and all different manners of things. She realized that thought was somewhat hypocritical as she looked down at her school attire. Whoever they were, they had something she needed. Gerti had been told it would be small - about the size of her thumb - and would have "V. 2.11" written on it. She was to retrieve this and take it back north for updating. She didn't know what it was or what they would be updating but the job paid enough that she wasn't concerned about it. That and she hadn't really been given a choice. It was either this or execution.

Frankly, she was glad the council offered to pay her at all. Everyone knows this part of the world is extremely dangerous and few were willing to even look at the job.

When she was younger, the rest of the children fawned over the adventurers who would come home covered in scars and telling wild stories. Gerti however, assumed that if they were getting injured so often they were probably bad at their jobs. Or at least they didn't come by their skills naturally - instead having to learn them in the harsh wasteland. Gerti had very few scars but the ones she had were pretty bad. She had one that spanned across her face, causing a gouge through her already rather flat nose.

These conflicting ideas and facts had always pissed her off because she felt she was fairly competent now. She had gotten the scar on her face from a chance encounter with a mutant in her teen years, when she was new to the wasteland, and she was lucky it hadn't killed her. Her other scar was a gash on her left arm that she received in the same attack. Her arm was in constant pain and the wound itself would still get infected if she didn't keep it clean frequently enough. It had been a mutant similar to the one she found just now - except its face had been more doglike with no features of a man remaining. For all she knew, it could've been an actual beast instead of a mutant. She tried to push those grim memories from her mind.

A group of Trustee-bots roamed the empty field. They were standard - four mechanical legs held up the mechanical torso of a human in the middle. They moved with spider-like grace - or at least she assumed they had when they were new. The torso being held up in front was supposed to look human, based on the posters she had seen of them hanging in various buildings and billboards on her travels.

This far gone, the fake skin had degraded and chipped off leaving nothing but the bare mechanical insides and support plates. Two of them were twitching in the rain as they walked their rounds. They all cradled long sleek rifles in their arms. She desperately wanted to use one but they only worked for the bots.

Groups of them continuously made rounds through the muddy field. She waited until she found a pattern in their patrols. A gap every fifteen minutes. The day had slipped away. Between the slow crawl through the city and now watching the bots navigate the fields.

Rain and cloud cover helped dusk arrive earlier than it should have. She either needed to get into the university or hunker down for the night. She waited for the Trustee-bots to cross a double-sided road in the middle of the field - heading north - before she made her way across the wide street and into the empty field. She traipsed through the mud and kept the patrols in the corner of her vision. She said a silent prayer of thanks for the loud rain to cover her noisy movement. She cleared a ditch that reminded her of a little creekbed outside Waco she would pass when hunting with her mother, and came up to a tall building.

The side was filled with windows and openings created by a century of neglect. She knelt down by a car, in the parking lot outside the building, and watched for patrols. Then she turned her attention to the windows. There was no sign of anybody watching. She hoped if there was anybody, she would be concealed enough by the rain.

"Do your duty, stay inside," said one of the Trustee Bots from an onboard loudspeaker. Gerti jumped. She knew this didn't mean anything but she was tense about being in the open.

From what she had gathered from her parents and the council, there had been a quarantine before the fires. The Trustee Bots had been conscripted and programmed to enforce the draconian laws. Anyone out past curfew would be shot on sight. After this long, the robots began to think anytime was past curfew. She made it across the field and into the lobby of a hopefully abandoned building.

The crevices of the space were filled with dirt and old world detritus. She found a placard on the wall that displayed a map of the university grounds. She traced her fingers along the glyphs until she found ones that included "D. O. R. M. S." There was another word in front but she was told it didn't matter. She was to find a room inside that building by the numbers two, zero, five. Inside she would find what she was after.

She thought about the layout of the buildings she had seen and used that to orient herself on the map. She then realized there was a star in that location and no other. She tucked that information away in her mind and left the lobby towards her next marker.

The announcements were still being made throughout the complex by unseen Trustee Bots. "D-d-do your d-d-d-uty, st-t-t-tay insid-d-de" - "Leisure hours are from nine A.M. to seven P.M." - "Please have a valid Government ID, along with Vector ID cards, available for inspection at all times."

One Trustee Bot tried to make an announcement but its speaker was so fried it came out as a buzz that sent shivers down Gerti's spine. According to her mental map, she was approaching the correct building. She stopped and hunkered down when she saw firelight flickering from one of the rooms on the third floor. She watched for a moment and only saw one shadow against the far wall. It was small and rocked back and forth rhythmically. It reminded her of the stories her mother had told her of witches.

She shook her head - she always did this to herself. She was tired from being on the road for so long. This was by the far, the furthest she had gone from home.

Again, she tried to push these thoughts out of her mind so she could think. She needed to reach the second floor and the rain should cover the sound of her movements from the floor below. Gerti watched the firelight and waited for any more movement.

The shadow eventually stopped rocking. The silhouette of a figure stood and walked to the window. It stood unmoving as it watched the black stone field where Gerti hid behind a burnt out car. Gerti thought there was truly no way it would be able to see her where she was.

After a few very uncomfortable minutes, the figure moved away from the window and disappeared out of view. Gerti let go of the breath she was holding. There were no stairs on the outside of the building but she saw an archway leading to a courtyard in the center. She cautiously entered.

"Please report any unsafe activity you may see from your fellow students," said a bot very close to her.

The words echoed from the courtyard and into the dark tunnel. Gerti froze. She could hear the clacking of the mechanical legs on the stone pavement. It was extremely close. She quickly drew her rifle from its cloth and leveled it at the exit of the tunnel. Her vision tunneled on the darkening evening light. She got a hold of herself and dropped down behind a bin that was against the tunnel wall. The rain was deafening. She peered past the bin and saw three Trustee Bots move past the opening - totally unaware.

"Please show identification," a cold voice said from behind her. She lost her balance and fell into the trash bin she was hiding behind - the plastic shell cracked when her shoulder rammed through it. As she fell, she got a look of the bot that had snuck up behind her.

"Please show identification and Vector ID" Its voice was cold and mechanical as it simultaneously raised its rifle. The weapon already had pinpricks of energy shimmering on its sides.

It was about to fire.

Gerti reached for her rifle to shoot back, or to run, or just do something. Her hand blindly grabbed it, accidentally pulled the trigger. A fireball lit the tunnel as the wayward bullet smacked into the stone wall across from her.

She felt something grab her by her shirt and drag her through an opening in the tunnel wall. A half second after, another flash of light exploded in the tunnel and the trash bin was a pile of molten plastic. The heavy door slammed shut in front of her and blocked her view. She was in complete darkness.

There were small metal clinking sounds from directly in front of her and she could hear someone shuffling around.

"Who are you?" Gerti asked in a panic. She was frantically feeling her pockets for a lighter she kept.

A small voice shushed her instead of answering. It wasn't calming.

She pulled out the lighter and struck the wheel. A momentary flash of light revealed a girl.

Another showed her getting closer. Another showed Gerti's rifle laying on the ground in front of a metal door with a mid-height bar across it.

The fourth strike lit the wet lighter.

The girl was kneeling beside Gerti. She was wearing hiking boots, dirty jeans, a dirty white t-shirt and her mousy brown hair was up in a ponytail. Her tanned face was covered in scars. Her arms were too. Gashes, gunshots, carved symbols. Each had healed over the white bumpy flesh that old wounds held.

Gerti panicked and dropped the lighter. She frantically crawled away in the dark. The floor was covered in the slick mud of rainwater and a century of errant dust.

The lighter flickered on.

The girl was holding it. Her horribly scarred face wore a smile in the wavering light of the small flame. The girl looked pretty young - maybe a few years younger than herself. Gerti figured maybe sixteen or seventeen.

"It's okay. I'm not going to hurt you," she said in a raspy voice that was still too gentle for her appearance.

Gerti stopped.

The girl stood up and offered Gerti a hand. After a few moments of rain soaked silence, she took it and stood up.

"Thanks for that," she said, gesturing towards the door. Gerti knew she would've been seeing the pearly gates if this girl hadn't've stepped in.

"No problem, it looked like you needed help."

"Well, you didn't have to and I appreciate it. I'm Gertrude - Gerti. What's your name?"

"I...I don't know," she answered.

The door handle began to rattle violently. The girl saw Gerti's expression when she looked at it.

"Don't worry. I locked it and they're not allowed to destroy school property. It's in their owner's contract."

"They blew up that trash bin just fine." Gerti said.

The girl thought for a moment.

"Probably just fulfilling waste disposal. Or they were aiming for you and didn't mean to hit the trash bin and for some reason that loophole works for them. Who knows?" The girl retrieved Gerti's rifle off the ground and held it out. "Nice rifle, is it a mosin?" she asked.

Gerti shrugged. She had gotten the rifle from her mother a long time ago. She never thought about it as having a model or manufacturer. It had always been a foundational truth in her life. Never having known another of its kind.

"It's a mosin," the girl said again with a smile. "Come on, I have a small fire upstairs and some towels to get you dry," she said as she started down the dark hallway. The lighter held a globe of soft firelight around her as she walked.

Gerti watched her closely in the darkness - she still wasn't a hundred percent sold. But again, she had stuck her neck out for Gerti and that meant something.

Gerti worked out that DORM must have been some sort of student housing back in the day. There were two single beds in each room she passed. She was surprised to see the amount of clothes and mattresses that had been left unraided in the past century. After a moment's consideration, she reasoned nobody was willing to risk certain death for a few stitches of century old threads and moldy mattresses.

The girl had set up a small fire ring next to a broken window. It was a wide pan set on a couple of cinder blocks.

"Are you alone here?" Gerti asked.

"No. I have a whole army of robots guarding me. Not to mention those maroon crew cut clones that patrol the area."

17

"The what?" Gerti asked.

"You haven't seen them? There's a group of guys here that are all buddy-buddy with those robots. They run that field every morning," she said, motioning towards the muddy field Gerti had crossed.

"The bots don't shoot them?" Gerti asked.

"I guess their papers are in order."

The girl rummaged around in a pile of clothes, pulled out a towel, smelled it, shrugged, and threw it to Gerti. Then the girl found some pants and a green flannel shirt and handed them over before sitting down at the fire with her back turned.

"So, what are you doing here, Gerti?" she asked with a friendly tone.

"I was hired to find something in the dorms. How long have you been here? Why'd you read the owner's contract?" Gerti asked, changing into the musty dry shirt. She looped her wet bear shirt into her belt.

"First, I've been squatting here for a few weeks. Second, I've been here for a few weeks," she laughed, "One of the students that lived here had the contract in his room and I got bored. What are you looking for? Maybe I can help."

"I don't know what you'd call it, but it's small and has V2.11 written on it. I was told to look around room two oh five." Gerti said.

"Well, let's go look. That's just downstairs," the girl said, getting up and heading for the door. She turned to make sure Gerti was following.

The two of them found the plaque that read *"205"* and underneath were two names: Collin G. Ferdinand and David E. Liebowitz. Gerti turned the metal handle but the door wouldn't budge. She backed up, placing her boot on the door by the handle and pushed with all her weight. The door was flexing in its frame but didn't give way.

The girl held up a hand. Gerti stopped trying to break the door. The girl pulled out a key and slid it into the door's lock. There was a satisfying clunk and the door swung open.

"Why didn't you do that from the start?" Gerti asked.

"I wanted to see if you could do it. It would've been pretty cool. This is actually the room that had the contract."

"Where'd you even get that key?" Gerti asked.

"I found it in one of the rooms when I first got here. I think it opens all the dorm rooms," she said. The girl held the lighter up and entered the room.

Aside from the layer of dust on everything, it looked mostly undisturbed. There were two single beds on either side of the small room, at the foot of each bed were two small desks. The far desk was covered in cans and plates, the one closest to the door was covered in burnt papers with an old personal computer resting on top. The computer lid was closed. It's case badly melted. Gerti pried it open, on the keys was a letter folded in thirds. Gerti picked up the computer and looked it over. V2.11 was nowhere to be seen. She did, however, see v2.13 written on a small rectangle of black plastic with a metal end. She picked it up and examined it for a moment before pocketing it. She picked up the letter and looked at the contents. None of the words landed with her, but she did see V2.11 written about half way down.

"Can you read?" Gerti asked the girl.

"Can you not?" the girl asked, grinning.

Gerti shook her head.

"Ugh, yeah, sorry. I can read," she said.

Gerti gave her the letter to examine.

"It's from one of Bryan's professors, to D. Liebowitz. It says he can't trust the eh-mail service to communicate and wants to meet in one of the libraries to discuss the update rollback," she said, clearly not completely understanding a lot of the words.

"Did it say which library?" Gerti asked.

"Evans. Room three twenty-four," the girl read off the letter.

"Do you know where that is?"

"Not off the top of my head but I bet we can find it. There's a map downstairs," she said, before starting towards the door.

The map downstairs was an exact copy of the one Gerti had seen outside. Gerti looked at the words "EVANS" and then looked at the map trying to match the letters. It was in a large section of buildings to their north.

"I'm going to head there now." Gerti said, "Thanks for saving me earlier, and for the clothes."

"Don't you want to wait for the morning?" the girl asked.

"The bots don't work as well in the rain. I need to take advantage of the weather while I can."

"That's fair. We'll be safer if we do it now," the girl said, hiking up her pants.

"You want to come with me?" Gerti asked, surprised.

"Well sure, I want to know how this ends. If I let you go by yourself, I'll probably never know why the professor couldn't trust their normal communication or what update they're rolling back. You've brought up a lot of questions that I want the answers to," she said.

"I could prolly use the help." Gerti said, thoughtfully.

"Two heads and all that," the girl said, smiling.

Gerti nodded.

They scavenged around the building until they found two coats with plastic exteriors. They had to dig under a pile of charred clothes to find some that were intact. The coats were too big for them but they'd keep the rain off. The coats were musty and smelled like a hundred years of dust and neglect.

The two girls went to the top of the building and looked over the edges to scout the surrounding area. There were several bots walking around the campus from their vantage point but none of them were next to the building they were hiding in. They went downstairs to the door facing the north, and pushed it open into the rain.

Chapter Two
September 23rd, 2114
College Station, Texas
Gertrude Alvarez

The rain continued to fall in a torrent as they stepped outside. They ducked their heads and bore the brunt of the water on their jackets' hoods.

There was a road running left and right and a large dorm building just in front of them. They took a left and made their way across the street. A concrete courtyard, with steps leading up to doors, had two Trustee Bots standing guard. The two girls dipped right into an alleyway between the two large buildings. Another concrete stairway took them through a glass covering. They rested for a moment in the dark causeway. To the north was a small parking lot and a covered sitting area.

"Watch behind us." Gerti told the girl. She turned around and watched where they had come from.

Gerti wasn't used to having another person with her but having someone to watch her back was kind of nice - a second set of eyes. After a minute of nothing but rain, Gerti was satisfied that the way was as clear as she could guarantee.

"Let's go," Gerti said.

The two of them made their way back into the rain and across another concrete courtyard towards another large building with a thousand dark windows.

Gunfire lit their surroundings as they passed into the parking lot.

"Present I-i-i-identif-f-fication," said a bot that had been motionless in the covered area.

"Run!" Gerti yelled, as bolts of energy zipped past them.

They ran as fast as they could through the rain slicked paved street towards the building to their left. Rain splashed underneath their boots like little meteor impacts. Gerti had prided herself on her speed when she was growing up. She was extremely thankful for this innate speed right now. More energy weapon shots lit the night and blast marks erupted on the building in front of them. They cast harsh lights that reflected off the rain soaked surfaces of the campus.

The girl let out an anguished scream from behind Gerti. She turned around to help the girl up, expecting her to have fallen. To Gerti's surprise, the girl was still on her feet running toward her. Shocked, Gerti turned back towards the building and kept running.

They made it to a set of metal double doors.

The girl threw one open and held it for Gerti to go in. Blast marks melted through the door as it closed. Molten metal splashed into the dark hallways.

The girl quickly pulled out a small tool, and a lighter, from her pocket. She lit the lighter and thrust the tool into a small hole on the mid-level bar handle that spanned the door. The bar popped out into position. The girl placed her hand flat on the door itself and pushed.

It rattled in place but didn't open. Satisfied, the girl quickly limped up a flight of stairs. A trail of her blood followed each step.

Gerti followed.

They ran into a room on the second floor and closed the door. It looked like a small meeting area with a large table in the middle. Most importantly, there were no windows. The girl hopped up onto the table and sat with her feet resting on a chair. From the knee down on her left pant leg was completely soaked in blood.

Gerti tried to roll up the leg of the girl's jeans but quickly realized she wasn't going to be able to access enough of the wound. She pulled out a small knife and held it to the jeans before looking up into the girl's face. She was clearly in pain but was trying not to show it. Her jaw was clenched and her face was tight.

She calmly nodded her head.

Gerti cut the jeans up past the knee.

The girl placed the lighter down onto the table so she could grip the edge with her entire being. Gerti ripped the denim into four pieces and tied the ends together to make a longer strip. Years of experience in her dad's clinic was really pulling its weight right now.

"Lift," Gerti said, as she slipped the fabric under the girl's left thigh. She tied the strip with the knot just on the inside of the inner thigh and pulled as tight as she could.

The girl yelped.

"You're gonna be alright." Gerti said.

The girl nodded and smiled through her grimace.

Gerti grabbed a pencil off the table, stuck it through the fabric under the knot, and twisted.

Another cry of pain.

Blood had soaked the girl's shoe and had started to fall onto Gerti's boots. An impressive amount of blood, Gerti thought. She took the two tails of fabric and used them to lock the pencil into place. The girl started laughing through her tears.

"What's funny?" Gerti asked.

"Just another scar for the collection," she replied.

"Dad would say you have a gallows humor." Gerti said through a chuckle.

"How's the leg look?"

"Not bad." Gerti lied.

"You haven't even looked at it," the girl said.

Gerti grabbed the lighter and held it closer to the wound.

The skin had been burnt away leaving an empty crater that exposed bone - fibia, tibia, tibular? Gerti couldn't remember, but it was the thin one in the back of the lower leg. The skin around the hole was black and charred. The wound extended from one side of her calf through to the other side.

Gerti wondered how the hell she had kept running with this. The tourniquet had slowed the bleeding but she would need serious medical help if she wanted to stay alive for more than a few days. Any infection would be the end of her and, judging by the uncleanliness of her jeans, an infection was almost a guarantee.

"Do you know any doctors in the area?" Gerti asked.

"The crew cuts probably have one. I haven't really seen any other people in town since I got here though. Wrap up my leg and I can keep going with you. I can barely feel it," she said.

"Your leg's in pretty bad shape." Gerti said, chuckling softly at the girl's defiance.

"I've had worse," she said.

"You haven't even looked at it."

The girl leaned forward to look at the missing chunk of leg. She grimaced and leaned back again. "I've had worse," she repeated. Gerti pulled out the cleanest shirt she had in her bag and wrapped the girl's calf.

"Okay, where are the crew cuts?" Gerti asked.

"There are more dorms to the west of where we were. I think it was labeled dorm one. Tell them it's for me - I've been trading with them. They seem nice enough," she said.

Gerti nodded. This girl had stuck her neck out on Gerti's behalf, it was time to repay that. Which was good in a way. She didn't like being in debt to people for too long.

"I'll be right back. Stay here." Gerti said.

The girl nodded her head before laying down on the table.

Gerti locked the door before shutting it. Her mission here was important but the timing wasn't. She only had a few hours before that tourniquet on the girl's leg caused serious damage to her. She had left the lighter with the girl so she carefully made her way down the dark staircase and into a lobby below. Very little light came through double glass doors.

Gerti went to the window and peered out. All she saw was rain and a little moonlight reflecting off metallic surfaces. She could see the glass causeway where they had been and she could see the covered sitting area where the bot had been hiding. She watched the street but there was no movement.

She slowly opened the door and made her way out into the rain. There were three almost identical buildings in front of her and then several large dorm buildings just past them. There were lights on in a few of the building's windows. She looked around at the others and didn't see any more lights. Gerti looked around, again, for the bots. There were none.

None that she could see anyway.

She made her way between two of the identical buildings and pushed toward the dorm. The lights were off on the first floor but she could see a solid metal door in the middle of the building. Looking around, she made her way to it. The wet handle rattled gently as she tried to open it but it remained locked.

She cursed for not taking the girl's keys. To her right was a window covered by long dead shrubbery. One last time, she looked around for bots. Not seeing any, she took the covered rifle out from under her arm and ran it through the window as hard as she could.

The shattering glass was deafening and she knew bots would be on their way. She broke as much as she could and climbed through the window. She cursed again as she cut her bare hands on the glass - it didn't feel too deep. And at least she fell onto a soft bed.

In addition to rainfall, she could hear the heavy clunking of the bots approaching. She sprang up and stumbled in the dark towards where the dorm room door should be. It opened without a fuss. She took the rifle

29

out of her oil cloth and pushed the cloth into a small bag on the back of her belt.

The hallway was almost completely dark. The only light came from dim moonlight through a few open dorm rooms. She very carefully made her way to the stairwell at the end of the hall.

Small lights flashed around the stairs and yelling came from the second floor. Gerti ducked behind a bench in the hallway and watched the staircase. The lights settled on the landing.

"Who's down there?" a man's voice called. A few long seconds passed before anyone else spoke.

"See, nobody's there. Just a window giving out to the wind," said a second voice.

"Shut up, the wind's not going to beat on a window fifteen times," said the first voice.

"Just tell us who you are!" called the first voice. Gerti took a deep breath, and leveled her rifle at the stairwell, just in case.

"My friend's hurt. She said she's the girl that's been trading with y'all," she called out. "She said y'all might have a doctor?"

"We do, is your friend with you?" called out the first voice.

"No, she's in a different building." Gerti answered.

"How'd she get hurt? Why were y'all out without your tags?" asked the second voice.

"One of the bots shot her in the leg as we were crossing the street. And we don't have tags." Gerti answered.

The lights began to move.

Two people shifted slowly into the landing and began scanning the light around the hallway. They must not have seen Gerti because the lights never settled on her hiding spot. One of the men's silhouetted chests rested squarely in her sights.

"Are either one of you students here?" asked the second voice. The voice belonged to the man in Gerti's sights.

Gerti didn't answer. She sat there motionless.

"If you're not a student of this university you can't get an identification tag. If you can't get one of those, you can't freely move through the campus. I'm sorry your friend got shot but that's the consequences of breaking the rules," said the same man.

Gerti took a breath - her finger started to squeeze the trigger out of anger but thankfully she was interrupted.

"Shut the hell up, Hughes," said a third, older voice. The third man came down the stairs. He had gray hair and was wearing a green jacket with tan pants that flared out at the hips and came back in by the knees with tall leather boots that went down from there. "Get that light out of my face," he said while swatting the young man's hand out of his direction. "We *will* help your

31

friend. Hughes, Jacob, go upstairs and get Clements," he said.

The two younger men quickly moved out of the stairwell. The older man flicked on a red light and moved down the stairs with a heavy limp.

"Pardon them their spirit," he said as he moved toward the bench. He stopped at the end of the seat, leaning on the arm rest and looking around the hall. He had glasses on and his gray hair was cut short.

"I'm here." Gerti said. The man's eyes flared as he looked down and saw the rifle barrel staring him in the chest.

"Yes, you are," he said, moving out of the gun's way. "Clements will help your friend. I would go but…" He gestured to his bum leg.

Gerti stood from her hiding spot and slung the rifle over her shoulder. The man had a white plastic card hanging from a cloth lanyard around his neck.

"Thank you. Do those tags keep the robots from attacking you?" she asked.

"That's what we found. Only during the day though. They still shoot at us if we go out at night," he said.

"Can I have a few?" Gerti asked.

"Absolutely not," the man said. "You'd have to be one of us and even then, you need to pass several trials. We also have fewer and fewer of them as the years go by."

Before Gerti could respond, a young man came bumbling down the stairwell and into the older man's light. He was tall and rail thin, with a square jaw. His hair was cut much shorter than the older man's.

"Howdy, I'm Clements. Hughes told me you have a friend that needs help. Where is she?" he asked, looking around the empty hall for her.

"She's not here, I didn't want to move her. Her leg is pretty torn up. I have a tourniquet on her femoral artery but I don't know how long that's going to keep her from bleeding out." Gerti said, already heading towards the door.

Clements followed her, hiking up a black fiber bag on his shoulder.

The door proved difficult to open as the storm had picked up. The rain came down at a hard angle and the wind whipped at Gerti's jacket. She turned around to make sure Clements was following her. They were both running through the street but the crashing sounds of the rain completely drowned out any footfalls.

Gerti quickly glanced around for bots but she couldn't differentiate any movement from the static of the rain. They made it past the three identical looking buildings. She hadn't been able to actually see them because of the haze of heavy rainfall. She had just known they were in this direction.

Through the heavy rain, she could barely make out the building that the girl was in. As they got closer,

33

Gerti saw the double doors she had exited were both open. She pulled the rifle off her shoulder and held it at the ready as they approached.

She would have to clean and oil her gun thoroughly if she made it through this. The poor thing, she thought. All her ammo was steel cased, so those would have to be cleaned and oiled as well to prevent rust. She worked the bolt back a little to make sure she still had a round chambered before closing it again.

Gerti took point as they entered through the open doors. She held the long rifle level as she scanned the small entryway and the small section of banister above them.

There was a click and a red light illuminated the entryway. Clements was holding an elbow flashlight that he clipped onto the front of his shirt.

"Please exit the facility and return to your hall." A robotic voice said from upstairs. Gerti quietly peered up through the stairwell. She could see one of the bots standing in front of the door where the girl was hiding.

Clements clicked the red light off before he entered the stairwell. Gerti was thankful he had some self-awareness. He came up the stairs behind her and placed a hand on her right shoulder. She aimed the rifle at the center mass of the robot's torso.

"We'll have to get in and move her somewhere else before you treat her." Gerti whispered to Clements.

She imagined this building would be swarming with bots after the gunshot. She couldn't see or hear a response from him but he patted her shoulder twice.

"Cover your ears," she whispered. She felt his hand leave her shoulder. She counted to five, tensed her head like her mother had taught her, and squeezed the trigger. Truthfully, that trick may have worked when firing the gun outside while hunting but inside the enclosed staircase the report from the rifle was utterly deafening.

The concussion rocked its way through her body and her ears lost the ability to hear anything but a high-pitched ringing.

The torso of the bot exploded into a storm of metal and sparks. It rapidly turned its mangled body towards the stairwell and raised its weapon towards Gerti. She quickly racked the bolt and fired a second time. The bot's weapon fragmented and an explosion of red energy knocked the bot into the wall and the door it had been speaking to. The two of them ran up to the damaged door. Pieces of plastic casing and metal frame protruded from the thin wood.

Gerti yelled that it was her before she tried the door. She could barely hear herself say it. The door was still locked for a few seconds until the girl opened it from the other side.

The girl and Clements exchanged words before he lifted her left arm over his head to support her. He clicked on the red light and the three of them moved west further into the building. Red and blue lights flickered inside the hallway through open classroom doors. They reached the end of the building and went down a flight of stairs.

They looked out the window in the top right of the door to make sure the street was clear. Red and blue lights were coming from their left where they had entered a minute ago. A loud crash echoed through the empty building as bots busted into the building.

The three of them pushed out into the heavy rain and took a right towards the next building. They found a front entrance into a small lobby that had several hallways leading off it. They picked one and moved quickly down it. They found a large empty room with long cubicle covered desks. Gerti and Clements lifted the girl onto one of the desks.

Clements clicked his flashlight to white and began undoing the bandage on the girl's calf. He grimaced at the wound then looked up at the girl and smiled.

Gerti could barely hear what he said to her. Something trying to be reassuring, she figured. Gerti watched as he pulled out a set of rags and a container of clear liquid, she figured alcohol, and began wiping blood away from the wound.

The girl screamed - that did break through the high-pitched whine of her ringing ears. She hated shooting indoors.

Clements took a strip of leather out his bag and handed it to the girl.

She nodded her head, put the strip between her teeth, and bit down.

Clements produced a small squirt bottle from his bag and started running liquid into the wound. Then he took a needle and thread and began stitching the wound closed.

The girl winced each time the needle and thread went into her skin.

Gerti moved to keep watch out the hallway and into the street outside. The lights came and went but the bots left their building alone.

After some time, the deafening ringing in her ears started to subside and she could hear the rain again. She could hear the girl's grunts of pain and she could hear Clements trying to comfort her. She could also hear the robots individually broadcasting a message.

"Remain where you are. There seems to be an active shooter on campus. Authorities have been alerted." The message was repeated by every bot that patrolled under the window.

"Where were they being charged?" Gerti thought. She knew there were batteries you could charge

with salt water but those weren't widespread at the time of the world's Rebirth.

Someone or something was keeping these things charged. And on top of that, they acted as a single unit. Gerti figured maybe each unit operated individually and then communicated to everyone in range but then there would have to be a hierarchy or else each unit's orders could be contradicted by another unit's orders.

So there was either a ranking hierarchy for the units, a priority list of certain orders, or there was a central unit that was receiving all the data and assigning bots to different situations. The last made the most sense to Gerti. She stepped back into the ad hoc operating room.

"Where do the robots go to recharge?" Gerti asked Clements.

"Academic Plaza" Clements said. "I'm assuming anyway. They all go there periodically, like a shift change. Will you hold the light?" he asked.

Gerti softly closed the door and tried to lock it but it was one of those doors with the bar across the middle and she didn't have that little key. She leaned the rifle against the wall, by the door, and moved a desk to block the entry. Then she went to help Clements with the light.

"That's a good tourniquet. Where'd you learn that?" Clements asked. His voice was slowed by his focus on the stitching.

"My mom and dad help people, and I helped them when I was younger." Gerti answered.

"That makes sense. In this day and age, I suspect most people would've put a bullet to her and moved on," he said while tying off a stitch and moving to the next.

"It would've been too loud." Gerti said, grinning.

"Yeah, then you'd have to deal with a bunch of frenzied murderous robots," the girl said, also grinning.

"Exactly." Gerti agreed. The truth was that the girl had saved her life less than twenty minutes ago and that endeared her to Gerti.

The front doors of their building opened and the heavy mechanical footsteps of a Trustee Bot echoed through the hallway.

"Remain where you are. There seemsssss to be an an an active shooter on campus. Authorities have been alerted." The robot struggled through the message. "We will be checking... computer labs... Please provide valid identification when asked."

"Did you lock the door?" Clements asked.

"No, I didn't have a key." Gerti answered.

The girl reached in her pocket and retrieved the small key. She held it out and Clements grabbed it before making his way to the door. The desk was shoved out of the way as the door swung open. A red beam of light emitted from the Trustee Bot that washed over the entire room before focusing down on Clements tag that hung from his neck.

"Instructor… Benitez… Is your class safe?" asked the bot.

Clements stared at the bot for a second. Gerti could see a small screen inside its chest that had something on it but she couldn't make out exactly what.

"Instructor Benitez, is your c-c-class safe?" the bot asked again.

"Yes. Thank you." Clements said.

"It's my p-p-pleasure." the robot said before pausing. "You are covered in blood. Mrs. Benitez. Are you sure your class is safe? If the active shooter is present, I am more than capable of assisting."

It scanned the room again and located the girl sitting on the desk. The bot pushed past Clements and approached the girl. Gerti stood up from behind the desk and moved towards the door. She tried to position herself between the bot and her rifle. The bot scanned the girl several times before turning back to Clements.

"Unknown ID: appears to have suffered a gunshot. Trustee Medibots have been alerted and are en route." The bot approached Clements. "Mrs. Benitez, please report how the student was injured."

Clements froze.

"Mrs. Benitez, r-r-report how the student was injured," the bot said again as it got closer to Clements.

"She was attacked by the shooter." Gerti said from beside the door.

"Yes. She was attacked by the active shooter. She came here looking for a place to hide." Clements said in a rush.

The trustee bot paused, a light came on at the end of a small antenna on its head.

"Understood. Did you get a good look at the shooter?" it asked.

"Uh, yeah." Clements began. "He was six feet tall, had blue hair, and was wearing one of those orange reflective vests."

The light on the antenna strobed for a few seconds then stopped.

"Thank you for helping. A description has been given to the other Trustee Bots." it said before walking towards the door.

It stopped as it was passing Gerti. Its head snapped towards the mosin leaning against the wall.

Red and blue lights flared to life and an alarm started wailing. It swung one of its arms at Gerti, knocking her away from the rifle and onto the ground.

Clements pulled a knife off his belt and jumped at the bot. It moved to dodge and put itself between Gerti and her rifle. Clements spun to face it.

Gerti stood up and noticed the antenna light starting to flash quicker. With the bot focused on Clements, she climbed onto the bot's back and snapped

41

the antenna. It bucked beneath her but she held onto the frame.

"Communication to the central hub lost," came from the bot's speaker as it reached for Gerti behind its back. Its torso swiveled around to face Gerti and one of its two front legs raised to keep Clements at bay.

With the bot's chest swiveled around, Gerti could see the little screen inside. It read "*V2.15 Running ASP. Running SDP.*" These symbols of course meant nothing to her.

One of its metal arms knocked her off its back and onto the ground, the other leveled its weapons at Clements and started to charge it.

Gerti landed hard, the breath knocked out of her.

Unfortunately for the Trustee Bot, she landed next to her rifle. From the ground, she grabbed it and aimed at the bot but the shot was blocked by Clements trying to stab at its chest.

"Move!" Gerti yelled.

Clements was too focused on dodging the bot's attacks and staying out of the weapon's muzzle. Gerti aimed at the underbody of the bot instead and pulled the trigger.

A geyser of sparks erupted from its belly. The bot's weapon fizzled out and it recoiled. She loaded another round into the chamber and aimed for its chest. Chips of metal and plastic flew out the back of the bot's chest as another round tore its way through.

It collapsed on the ground and writhed wildly. Clements approached it, took a bundle of wires in his hands, and severed them with his knife. Its movement stopped.

A moment later, an oscillating warble came into the hallway.

"Help is on the way, Mrs. Benitez!" said a chipper female voice.

Gerti quickly hid on the other side of the classroom. She unloaded the last round inside the internal magazine before retrieving a clip from her belt pouch and shoving five fresh rounds into place. She thought about discarding the rifle and staying with Clements and the girl but she wanted to keep the rifle near her in case the new bot tried to kill them too.

A white Trustee Bot with a red cross painted on its chest walked into the classroom. Its case was much more intact than the others, the paint was barely chipped. It had a manufacturer's mark that read "*Treighl Robotics MU-1274*" and the plastic shell that made them look human was still doing the job. It had a bright white light on its chest and soft white lights at various points around its body that pointed down onto the ground but most importantly, it wasn't carrying a rifle.

"Dear me," it said, looking at the destroyed bot on the ground, "What happened to him?"

"The shooter got him," the girl said from the desk.

The bot approached her slowly. One of its hands plugged into a port on its back and attached to a canister of something.

"Then he died doing his duty to the student body. Did you see which direction the shooter went?" asked the robot. Its canistered arm slowly swung in front of its body and moved towards the leg. Its other arm lifted the leg and held it up into white light.

"He said something about going to the golf course." Clements said. The antenna on the bot's head started blinking as it undoubtedly started broadcasting the new information.

"Hopefully our boys can stop them before anyone else gets hurt. Mrs. Benitez, did you do these stitches? They're beautiful," it said. It placed the canister just above the wound and said "Okay dear, this may sting a little." A yellowish white foam fizzled out of the canister as the bot moved along the wound's length. The girl winced for a moment but then relaxed. The bot turned her leg over and did the other side as well. It swapped out the canister for another. The bots arm whirled around the injured leg leaving it wrapped in bandages.

"You should be right as rain in a few days. Just try to stay off it as much as you can." It turned to Clements, "Mrs. Benitez, is there anything else I can do to assist your class?"

"No, that was it. Thank you," he said quickly.

"Of course, it was my pleasure. Stay in your classroom until the shooter situation has been resolved," it said, before making its way towards the door.

It stopped at a trash can, a small port opened on its torso, and two small canisters discharged into the bin, then it exited left down the hallway. They stood quietly, listening to the heavy footsteps until the bot had left the building.

"Did you know they had medics?" Gerti asked as she approached Clements and the girl.

"I had no idea," he said. He walked over to the trashcan and pulled out the two canisters.

"Tissue reproduction medgel. Expiration, one nineteen, twenty-twenty-seven," he read off one, he held up the other, "Gauze wrap." He laughed and threw them both back into the trash.

Gerti felt a rock in her shoe. She sighed, annoyed. Now wasn't the best time to clear a rock from her shoe but it definitely wasn't the worst.

"Hang on," she said, sitting down in one of the chairs to deal with it. She took her bloodied boot off to find the pebble. She hadn't felt it earlier, but maybe she was just focused on everything that was happening.

Gerti felt around her matted sock and remembered that the girl's blood had soaked into her boots. She pulled a fresh pair of socks out of her bag and began changing them. She felt the rock inside her sock. But it didn't fall out like she was expecting.

It clung to the cloth.

"Hey, can I see that light?" she asked Clements. He came over with white light and gave it to her.

The rock that clung to her blood-soaked sock was a crimson red crystal.

Chapter Three
September 22nd, 2114
Bryan, Texas
Joseph Marion

Joseph cursed as he quickly pulled his left hand away from the circuit board. A blank spot on the blue PCB had Treighl Robotics printed in bold cream letters. Joseph was extremely thankful this was one of their simpler boards that didn't have any complicated programming attached. A few years ago, he had tried to fix a faulty loading arm control board on a tractor Danny Carregan had found at an old construction site. A week of trying to reprogram the arm only achieved two things: Frustrating Joseph and bricking the control board.

The programming language Treighl used was called Amara+. The sections were incredibly well labeled but none of the individual lines made sense to Joseph. He was able to connect the arm to a simple control box he had made using a bunch of relays and micro switches. But man, that was a rough week.

Joseph yelped.

A sharp tingling sensation bounced around in his arm for several seconds before dying down. Evidently, one of the capacitors on the board still held a charge. He took a screwdriver that was wrapped almost entirely in electrical tape. The tip of the screwdriver was exposed and an insulated wire was wrapped around the shaft. A metal alligator clip was attached to one end of the wire, the other end was attached to the metal underneath the tape.

Joseph took the wire and clipped it onto the metal shelf near his work station. He then took the screwdriver and touched every single set of pins on every capacitor he could find. The board was fairly small - three inches by six inches. It was the charge control board off one of the small solar panels that had gone out. The mayor had asked him to take a look at it.

Joseph barely knew anything about them but he said he would try. After discharging all the capacitors, for sure this time, he flipped the board back over and looked at all the components. The larger components were mostly transformers and capacitors - they all looked fine.

Well, turning them over under the light, he could see some damaged plastic on one of the transformer brackets. Joseph tested the transformer windings with a small multimeter sitting on his desk. The reading on the screen read 0.0.

He laughed and shook his head before changing the dial from VDC to 20k Ohms. There we go. The digital readout displayed 10... 13... 15... O.L. Okay...

He turned the dial to 100k Ohms and tried again. The reading maxed out at OL again. He tested one of the undamaged transformers to make sure. The readings on all the others read as less than 1 Ohm. He cursed and dropped the board onto the table as another capacitor discharged into him. He shot up, kicked his chair, and took a deep breath.

Looking at his wrist watch told him he'd been working on the various boards for several hours now. It was almost midnight. He took another deep breath and returned to his work station. He picked up the damaged board and compared it to the good one he had there for comparison. It looked like a simple transformer. He'd work on this tomorrow. He had hope since he had at least found the issue with the unit but now he'd have to start the process of finding a replacement. Something that was almost entirely impossible since the Rebirthing fires. Everything paper, wood, or plastic that was left on the surface burnt away. Joseph lived in the ruins of an old city's downtown district that was made of brick and concrete.

His great-great-grandparents had taken shelter in a Diurnal Co. shelter and his grandparents had come out of it into this world. The shelter had been built several miles outside the old city limits. It was a ten mile trek to its gate from here. A small staff of people stayed in the shelter to produce food for the expanding population outside. He had grown up there the same as most of the people in Bryan.

His older brother had been killed in a shootout when Joseph was around fourteen. He had traveled here with a settlement group not long after. Joseph walked to his window and watched the hurricane winds blow rain through the streets and against the buildings. Lightning struck on the western horizon. Joseph started to count the distance but the thunder hit almost immediately. Several more close lightning strikes preceded a falter in the room lighting. Another strike and the lights went out.

"Mrow?" Asked Purcevale, Joseph's gray two tailed cat.

"I know." Joseph said. He had pushed to combine the systems to cut down on the amount of wiring they'd have to do to make it work. And he figured connecting the batteries would help with the drain rate. Allen told him it'd be disastrous if the system ever failed but Joseph was the one doing a majority of the work. So he had wired it how he wanted it. He was looking forward to catching hell from the repair team in the morning. That was a problem for tomorrow's Joseph.

"Mroow." Purcevale declared.

"I know I'm an idiot. Thanks." Joseph said as he felt around on the workstation for his light. He felt the heat of the now cooling soldering iron and moved away from that. Screwdriver, charge control board, multimeter, headlamp. He pulled the headlamp over his head and pressed the button on top. A light sprang to life. Purcevale was looking up at him from the workstation. Joseph scratched the cat's head for a few seconds. Purcevale closed his eyes slowly and flicked both of its tails.

"I've got a long day ahead of me. So I'm going to sleep. Bud." Joseph fell onto his couch by the window where he slept. He sighed before getting up and checking the lock on his door. He returned to the couch in his small apartment, settled in, closed his eyes, and listened to the heavy storm outside. Purcevale jumped onto Joseph's chest and laid down. *'Shit, the food storage will be out all night,'* he thought. *'Aaaand I do have the spare board here.'* He cursed to himself again and threw the blankets off.

"Mrow!" Purcevale complained.

"Sorry, Chief. I gotta fix this." Joseph said. He turned on his headlamp, packed the good board into his tool bag, and threw it onto his shoulder over his coat.

"Hold down the fort while I'm out." He made his way out of the apartment, down a flight of stairs, and into the dark rainy street heading towards the town hall and the parking garage across the street from it. He made his way up the parking garage stairs to where they kept the solar arrays. Thunder boomed nearby and shook Joseph's chest and made his ears ring.

He fought against the door at the top of the stairwell that led to the roof. It opened and he could see the solar panel battery units under their covered area. They were still smoking.

A solid stream of swearing could be heard as he ran over to the units, pulling them apart. He pulled the units into the covered area so the rain wouldn't get into the circuits as he worked on them. He was able to find a handful of good batteries and connect them in a good harness that led to a charge controller. Then, he found the connector leading to the refrigeration and plugged it into the battery harness. The voltmeter on the board read 120v.

'Ok, that should work for a while,' he thought. He looked down at his watch - 1:07am. He jacked his jaw yawning. Had that really taken an hour?

"Hey Joe, you awake?" the radio in his bag went off. It was Allen.

"Yeah, Allen, I'm working on the solar units. I got one up and running." Joseph said.

"That's awesome. Jacob radioed me and said the power was out. Can you hook up the good one to the refrigerator?" Allen asked.

"'Course, I already have it hooked up." Joseph said.

"Great, I'll let Jacob know so he can tell the mayor." Allen said, "Go home and get some sleep."

Allen wasn't officially their boss but he had been doing this gig for the longest and had seniority. He had also been one of the reasons Joseph came to Bryan - Allen and his brother had been best friends growing up and losing him would've seemed like losing another brother.

"Will do." Joseph said. He waited for a second, to see if Allen would say anything else, before turning the radio off. Out of curiosity, he looked at the other charge control boards. They all had a few transformers that should replace the damaged one on the other board. He'd work on that tomorrow.

He walked home in the heavy rain, dried off, and collapsed on his couch.

The next morning, he packed up his things and went down to the town hall in the rain. The large glass and concrete building was the old town's courthouse. He passed a sign with a cartoonishly evil mutant attacking a woman in a blue sundress. The mutant had giant scorpion pincers for arms and its head was replaced with a rattlesnake about to strike.

Judy, the mayor's assistant, was bundled up in a blanket behind her metal desk in the lobby of the town hall.

"Everyone else is on top of the parking garage," she said.

"Thanks, Judy." Joseph said as he turned around and headed across the street to the garage.

He ran into Lucas on the way out of the town hall. Lucas was a little taller than Joseph and was new to the team. He had been part of the town guard until he fixed the ignition sequence board on one of their electric vehicles. The mayor and Jacob, the head of the guard, referred him to Allen to use. Joseph told him they were already in the garage. They walked together.

"Hey, 're you going to fix this?" Lucas asked.

"The power?"

"Yeah, the power." Lucas said, mocking him.

"I'm gonna try." Joseph said.

"Just curious, since it's your fault and all." Lucas said without the hint of a smile.

Joseph clenched his jaw and looked at Lucas in the eyes.

"That's why I came out here last night in the rain and got part of it up and running. What were you doing?" He asked, before climbing the stairs again.

"I was at home peacefully not breaking it in the first place."

They got to the second to highest floor and saw their team already pulling apart the boxes from the roof. Allen and Gloria were bent over a table examining the blackened boards. Allen was frowning and shaking his head slowly. Gloria was a small framed young woman who usually put the other members of the team to shame in terms of what she was willing to do to fix things.

'She probably pulled all these boxes down here before the sun came up.' Joseph thought with a smile.

"Sorry we're late." Joseph said.

"No worries." Allen said, "You know what was wrong with this setup?" He asked, looking at Joseph.

"Yeah Allen, I know. The systems were linked and the lightning fried everything at once." Joseph said.

"So maybe next time, we should separate them so this doesn't happen." Allen said.

"Yeah, maybe." Joseph said quietly.

"Just yeah. No maybe." Allen said, before taking a deep breath. "It's fine though, we'll figure this out. Thanks for coming up here last night to get the refrigeration hooked up," he said.

Joseph pursed his lips and nodded.

"The broken board I was working on just needs a transformer swapped out. I saw some good ones on these boards last night. We should be able to get a second bank working." Joseph said.

He heard some heavy breathing coming from the stairwell. He turned and saw their mayor, Frank, and his youngest son, Timothy, finishing the last flight of stairs. Frank was a thin man in his early forties and was wearing one of his usual solid color button up shirts. He had a canvas bag thrown over his shoulder and the son was carrying a plastic bag.

"We thought we'd bring breakfast. Allen, it was a good call keeping the refrigerators running." Frank said.

"It made the most sense. Joseph actually had the same idea and was hooking it up before I even talked to Jacob last night." Allen said.

The mayor looked at Joseph with a 'how 'bout that' expression.

"Is that right? Well, good work Joe," he said.

"Thanks, Frank." Joseph said, glad to be recognized.

The mayor set the canvas bag on the table and pulled out a couple jugs of water. Timothy pulled out some closed containers of hot soup. Gloria and Lucas went over and started eating with Frank and Timothy. Allen pulled the charge control board out of the box and turned it over in the light.

"I'm sorry." Joseph said quietly when he got closer to Allen.

"Like I said, it's okay. We'll figure something out. We always do, right?" Allen said.

"I think we have enough batteries to get another one setup - once we get the other board fixed." Joseph said.

"That's a good start but we still need, maybe three times even that to get the town back to where it was." Allen said. "Not to mention the expansions to the town that Frank wants to implement."

"We could set up wind generators." Lucas had walked over with his soup.

"Yeah, my family has some set up on their land. We could get their help." Gloria said.

"That'd be pretty nice." Allen said, "we could diversify where our energy's coming from."

"What about the Trustee Bot units at the old university?" Joseph asked. "They use Treighl batteries and Treighl chargers. I bet they even have solar cells."

The rest of them looked at Joseph in silence.

"Yeah that's true." Allen said. "They'd kill you before you could haul anything out of there though. Let's focus on less dangerous options first."

"I actually think that would be a pretty good idea, if we had enough people to spare. Joe going in by himself would be suicidal." Lucas said.

"Well, anyway. I like the wind idea. Let's save the Trustee Bots for another day." Allen said. "How about it, Frank. What do you think about getting some wind generators set up?"

"I like it," he said. "Gloria, would your family be willing to come in and help?"

"I can ask them." she said, shrugging. She didn't look too happy about the prospect, despite the fact she had offered.

Lucas and Timothy left the parking garage after everyone was done with the soup. The repair team spent most of the day rigging the second solar unit to be separate from the first.

Joseph and Gloria walked down to the commons to make sure the power actually turned on there. It was an old shop from when the town was young. The windows had long been replaced with pieces of sheet metal nailed and riveted into place. They walked in the front door and saw several families sitting at tables playing cards.

Gloria smiled and waved at Danny Carregan and his family. They were taking a break from their attempts at farming the plot of land they had claimed outside of town.

Joseph and Gloria walked into a dark backroom, opened the breaker boxes, and flipped all the breakers off.

"Breakers 're off." Gloria said over the radio.

"Alright, give us a second." Lucas responded. They waited in the dark closet at the back of the shop.

"How're you doin' with all this, Joseph?" Gloria asked.

"Mm'lright."

"Okay." Gloria chuckled softly.

"Hey, are you talking to your folks again?" Joseph asked.

Gloria hadn't spoken with her parents in several years now. There had been some hairy todo about her staying on the farm and helping them. Joseph always thought that sounded reasonable - especially when the alternatives were working repairs for the mayor in Bryan or braving the wastes. He figured she just wanted some space from them and didn't care where that put her.

"No?" Gloria replied.

"Then why'd you agree to talk with 'em about the wind generators?"

"I don't know. I didn't really want to… but you know how it is with Frank - it didn't feel like I could say no to him."

"You offered though?" Joseph reminded her.

She paused to think for a second before shrugging.

The mayor had that effect on people. Joseph couldn't explain it past him effectively owning the whole town. It always felt different than an authority thing though - Joseph never could really put it into words.

"Y'all try 'em now." Lucas crackled over the radio.

Gloria flipped the main breaker then flipped another couple smaller ones. Joseph popped his head out of the closet and saw the hallway light flickering to life.

"It's on." Gloria repeated the news through the radio.

"Go ahead and flip the breakers for the front." Allen said over the radio.

Gloria found the breakers labeled "storefront" in pen on taped down paper. A few people in the front made excited noises. They closed the closet and walked out to them.

"Okay, the refrigerators and this room have power. We're going to leave the rest off until we can get more power coming in." Joseph said.

"Thanks Joe, Gloria." Danny said.

"'Yeah, 'preciate it, y'all." Janet Laredo said from the other table.

"'Course." Joseph said as he stepped outside under the covered walkway.

The small downtown section reminded him of the old cowboy books his dad would read to him. A main street flanked by solid walls of brick buildings. There were a few streets off Main and they looked about the same.

"Y'all need us to come back up?" Joseph asked on the radio.

"Nah, I don't think there's much else we can do up here. When the storm's done, we can go out to Gloria's place and talk to her folks." Allen said back, "In the meantime, just see what there is around town we can fix."

"Y'sir." Joseph responded. He turned the radio off. Gloria was looking up at him.

"Don't go to the university. Not by yourself anyway," she said.

"But if I do, will you watch Purcevale?" he asked.

Gloria frowned but nodded.

"Do you still have my key from last time you watched him?" he asked.

She reached into a pocket and pulled out a set of keys. There had to be fifty keys on it but she was holding the key to his apartment.

"I swear. There are more keys every time I see that thing," he said, laughing. She smiled.

Joseph spent the rest of the day plugging leaks around various people's windows and sealing door frames. Rain like this usually only came once a year and usually signaled a change in temperature for the cooler. Joseph was always thankful for that. His mind spent the rest of the day beating himself up about the battery banks and the solar arrays.

Well, it flipped between that and thinking about colder weather and snow. The cowboy books, from his childhood, always mentioned the snowy mountains of Colorado and Montana. Joseph had obviously never actually experienced snow. He'd been inside the shelter's walk-in freezer but that was as close as he had gotten. The weather in this part of the world usually consisted of low "one-teens" to mid one-twenties during the day and mid-fifties at night.

Never snow though.

There were a lot of things in those books Joseph had never experienced. Things like trees, wild horses, cattle drives, shoot outs, river boats, banditos, or indians. Well, he'd been present for a shootout but he was too young to have participated. Come to think of it, he had experienced banditos at the same time.

Okay, snow, trees, wild horses, cattle drives, riverboats, and indians. Although there were a few families in the shelter that had native american ancestry.

Joseph shook his head - he was stalling.

He looked over what he was taking. Headlamp, flashlight, tourniquet, screwdriver bit set, multi-meter, small bottle of gun oil, pistol, a couple spare magazines, and his radio. His heart was pounding thinking about doing this. He took a deep breath and packed all his stuff into a small shoulder bag, except for his pistol, which went into a leather holster on his beltline. He practiced drawing it a couple times at himself in his bathroom's mirror.

'You're stalling again, Bud,' he thought. He pulled the slide of his 1911 back, just enough to make sure there was a round in the chamber, and holstered it.

"Gloria'll be by to keep you fed. Don't expect more than that though. I'm pretty sure she's allergic to you." Joseph said while petting Purcevale, who was lounging on a crumpled up shirt by the door.

He checked his watch, 6:17pm, and stepped outside.

The rain had died down a little but the wind had picked up. It ripped at his coat as he walked down Main. He approached the sheet metal fence that had been built around the old downtown district to keep out the roving Trustee Bot patrols.

There was a gate. Willow and Miguel were both manning it from a small stone tower built into their perimeter wall. Must've been the rare date night for them. Frank was in the process of making enough concrete to build the entire wall out of stone but that took time and a lot of limestone.

The gate in the metal fence was on wheels and the guard on duty would have to come down and unlock a padlock to get it open whenever anybody entered or exited. Really, the fence wouldn't have kept out anybody with an ounce of determination but it looked good for when elections rolled around.

He thought about just asking Willow and Miguel to let him out through the main gate - he'd been friends with them growing up - but it was already past dusk and it was against the law to leave city limits after dark.

Willow laughed about something Miguel said.

Joseph slipped down an alley and behind the barbershop to a place in the fence with a loose piece of sheet metal. He had to move a board and pull the metal back but he got through.

The world outside the walls was more bleak than inside. Most of the buildings out here were old homes built in the 1940s. Which is to say, there were no buildings anymore - just debris and cracking foundations.

He walked long enough down Main Street that he knew Willow and Migual wouldn't investigate too hard if they saw someone. He turned on his flashlight and walked towards the university. Joseph stayed on the sidewalk as much as he could. There were some building ruins out here and he wanted to have access in case someone ambushed him. Not that it was likely, there really weren't that many people living in this area anymore. Really it was just the Cadets and his little town. Neither of the groups were really large enough to have the outcast population necessary to support roving bandits.

Predators were a concern though, mutated or not. Ranging from feral dogs all the way to the mutated coyotes, boar, and of course tigers. Hell, the university even had the Trustee Bots and he knew those were a lot more dangerous than feral dogs.

The Trustee Bots would occasionally patrol the streets of the old cities. They could usually be avoided though. He figured it would take about an hour and half to get to the university. The rain suddenly picked up again. The bag would protect the radio and headlamp but he dreaded the rust on his pistol. He picked up the pace and started jogging. He finally made it to the ruins of the old bar district. There were four Trustee Bots patrolling the courtyard between the majority of the old bars.

"Please be able to p-p-provide valid identification and vector cards at any time."

"Remember, drinking and driving kills."

"Remember, only ten occupants aaaaare allowed inside a facility at any g——iven time."

He gave the old bar district a wide berth. There was a stone church nearby that had a fairly intact roof. He dipped inside the open doorway. The sanctuary was dark and filled with debris. He found a side room with a door and sat down for a quick rest. It was 8:12. He leaned his head against the wall and his eyes started closing themselves. Weirdest thing.

Rapid gunshots jolted his eyes open. They weren't close but there were a lot of them. They were high pitched and whiny like energy weapons.

'Some foolhardy explorer wandered too close to campus.' The irony of the thought wasn't lost on Joseph. However, maybe this was the distraction he needed to slip past the Trustee Bots.

He got to his feet and went back out in the rain. He carefully made his way towards campus. It was dark but he didn't want to alert the Trustees with his flashlight. As he was crossing the street, he heard the heavy footsteps of a Trustee a couple dozen yards to his left. He looked and saw a small square light moving in the darkness about eye level with him. He slowly got down and hid behind a burnt out truck that had long been abandoned in the middle of the road. The light was moving towards him. He watched, hoping it would veer off but it stayed the course.

Joseph got down on all fours and crawled under the front of the car. The water running down the street flooded into his clothes and soaked him to the marrow. He just laid there and accepted his new reality for the next few minutes.

A bright red light flickered and scanned a car a few yards away. From his hiding spot, he could see the Trustee Bot examining the inside of the car.

His radio squawked from inside his bag.

"Hey guys," it was Allen calling, "If you're free, I was thinking y'all could come over to my place and we could hangout - relax for a bit. We've all had a rough day and I think we could use it."

The Trustee Bot snapped to attention and began moving towards Joseph's hiding spot. Joseph tried to get to his radio but his bag was by his side and there wasn't enough room under the truck to maneuver with it.

"Sure boss. Me and Krystal will head over." Lucas said.

"What about you Joe?" Allen asked.

"Joseph said he was feelin' sick. I'll swing by and see if he's doin' better." Gloria said.

'God bless her. Not that it will matter in a few more seconds.'

"Thanks Gloria." Allen said.

The Trustee Bot scanned the truck and waited a couple seconds before it started spreading its four legs out to look underneath. Joseph drew his pistol and pointed it around where he thought the bot would appear. Two more gunshots rang out. These reports had some meat on their bones - like a good sized rifle. Red and blue siren lights flashed to life on the Trustee Bot.

"Please remain inside. There is an active shooter on campus," said the Trustee Bot, as it ran towards the gunshots.

Joseph was one hundred percent sure the bot was less than ten seconds from shooting him. So again, the irony was not lost.

He waited for a minute before sloshing out from under the truck - his entire body coming down from the rush of adrenaline. He shakily pulled the bag off his shoulder and turned the radio off.

'At least laying in the river didn't destroy the radio. Silver linings and all that,' he thought.

He'd also have to remember the active shooter in all his future prayers.

Chapter Four
September 22nd, 2114
College Station, Texas
Gertrude Alvarez

Gertrude plucked one of the crimson beads off her sock and compared it to the ones inside the little pouch in her bag. They were identical.

"Are you a mutant?" she asked the girl.

"I don't think so. I don't know," she said, "If I am, I don't know what my mutation is."

"Has your blood always done this?" Clements asked. He was ruffling through the old shirt that Gerti had used to bandage her. He pulled out a small crimson bead.

"Yeah. Well, for as long as I can remember anyway," the girl said.

Gerti rolled the red crystal bead between her fingers. She handed it to the girl.

"I would feel weird holding onto this." Gerti said.

Clements agreed and passed on the one from the bandage.

"Thanks," she said.

"Don't spend 'em all in one place." Clements said.

The girl smiled.

Gerti had dealt with her fair share of homicidal mutants but she had met several that were just normal people. This girl seemed like the latter to Gerti.

Clements helped the girl off the desk and the three of them moved into the hallway. They worked through the building moving as northward as they could. They eventually came to an exterior door that opened to a small concrete walkway between large patches of bare mud.

There was no sign of the flashing lights, so they moved outside and across the open ground. They made it inside.

Gerti quickly scanned the room with her rifle. It was a large open room with tables and chairs randomly scattered about. There were books in various stages of fire and water damage. Several of the windows along the outside wall were broken and wisps of violent water were whipping in. They found a building map and located room 324. It was listed as being on a "quiet floor."

They carefully walked to the room, watching the shadow corners for movement. It was a small room with a window and a glass door that opened into the hallway. The window was broken and the room's table was upright leaning against the wall opposite from the door.

There were also three Trustee Bots laying motionless in front of the door in the hallway.

Gerti squatted over one. Its head had been blown to pieces. She lifted it to get a better look and it began twitching. In a static filled whisper it said,

"Aag Temhandi aah venaht... E.T.A... ten minutes. Firestorm inbound. E.T.A. ten minutes. Seek i-i-i-imediate shelt-" The unit stopped moving. Its artificial muscles went slack.

"What language was that? And was that from the fires?" Clements asked.

"I don't know." Gerti said. She lowered the head back onto the ground. She stood and tried to open the door to the study room. It was unlocked but opened outward into the heavy bots on the ground.

"Ah." She said quietly.

"Want help moving them?" Clements asked.

"I'll just go in through the window." She answered. Gerti moved towards the window and saw that the glass was broken outward into the hallway. There were pieces of glass all over. She slung her rifle on her shoulder and peered into the room. It was almost entirely empty except for a leather satchel lying on the floor at the base of the window and a corpse in the far corner. Its clothes were almost entirely threadbare and its skin was dried to its bones. There were bullet holes in the wall all around the corpse.

That guy wasn't a problem so she turned her attention back to the satchel. She had to balance herself on the window frame but she was able to reach it. It was stained dark brown and the leather was stiff and cracked. There was a brass placard on the front that was engraved with "*D. L. E.*"

"What'd you find?" the girl asked.

"David's bag, I think." Gerti answered. She opened the satchel and thumbed through the contents. Nothing labeled v2.11 - just a bunch of papers and a few notebooks. One of them had a black leather cover. She threw the bag over her shoulder to go through later.

"How far could he have gotten in ten minutes?" asked the girl.

"Who are y'all talking about?" Clements asked.

"David Liebowitz. He was a student here." Gerti said.

"Like, in twenty-four?" Clements asked.

"Yeah."

"That's a pretty cold trail. But that might help." Clements said, pointing his flashlight at a dark stained trail leading down the hallway. Gerti smiled.

"Three heads are better than two," she said.

The three of them followed the drops of stained carpet downstairs and through the building heading west. It ended at the doors going outside into a courtyard. The glass door was busted and bullet impacts marked the stone door frame.

"Shine your light over there." Gerti said, pointing to a door into the building across the courtyard.

He shined the light in that direction and Gerti could make out more bullet marks. The glass on the door was also shattered.

They looked both directions in the courtyard and didn't see any flashing lights. Clements' fake tip must have worked. They slowly moved into the courtyard.

The building across from them had a large ornate green dome in the middle. On top of the dome was a tall antenna tower. Once they made it to the shatter door, they saw the dark stain continue. They followed the stain up three flights of stairs. The drops and puddles turned into a long dragging stain that ended on the other side of a closed door.

"A supply closet?" Clements asked.

"I guess." Gerti said. She gently tried the handle on the door. It opened without much effort.

Inside, there was a corpse curled up in the corner in a fetal position. A student ID was laid around the corpse's neck and its right arm was wrapped around a large piece of metal.

"Is that a dog?" the girl asked.

"What? I doubt it." Clements said.

Gerti bent down to get a closer look. The piece of metal had an inscription on the sides. "*Trooper Mk*

IIIV" The first two I's were crossed out with red paint and the V was painted on. There were joints and it did look like it had limbs but they were completely rusted.

She reached past it to retrieve the ID badge.

The rusted metal moved. It lifted a canine-like head and opened its mouth like it was barking. It fought against the rust.

"It's okay, Buddy," she said, as she grabbed the ID. It was covered in a century of dust. But there it was, clear as day. The same name as on the dorm room's sign. She also noticed something odd in the corpse's skeletal hand.

She moved it aside and saw the little device with "*V2.11*" hand written on the side.

The metal dog snapped to bite her hand but ran out of power half way. Its head slumped and lightly landed on its intended target. She ran her hand over its metal ears and stood up. The device in David's hand was the same as the one she had found earlier.

"I think I found it," she said, turning it over to examine it.

"What's the plan now?" the girl asked.

"Sleep." Gerti said, nodding her head. "Sleep and then I'm headin' to turn this in."

She put the device in her ammo pouch, and looked at the ID. The girl looked at it too. The black and white photo was of a young man wearing glasses. He smiled, his whole future ahead of him.

"David Liebowitz. AI Engineering. Trustee Tech," the girl read aloud.

"Do y'all want me to hang around tonight?" Clements asked.

"We'll be fine if you want to head back," the girl said.

"Well, honestly, I don't want to go back at night. Not with the bots in a tizzy. I'd rather wait 'til morning so my badge'll mean something," he said.

They found a classroom. It was dimly lit by Clements' flashlight. He helped the girl into one of the few chairs that looked sturdy enough to hold her. There was a ring of dilapidated tables along the outside of the room and a table near the front. Clements started casually digging through the desk at the front of the room.

There were a few backpacks laying around the tables. Evidently, some of the students left in a hurry when they heard a wave of fire was about to roll through town.

The jacket had done a pretty good job of keeping Gerti's shirt dry but her pants were soaked. She took them off and laid them over a chair to dry overnight - the bloodied socks and her current socks went next to the pants. She made sure neither Clements or the girl were looking at her before she slid the v2.11 into a backpack that was sitting in the corner. Then she found a chair that looked sturdy enough, moved it over beside the girl, and sat down.

"What do you mean you don't know your name?" Gerti asked the girl.

"What?" she asked.

"Earlier. I asked you what your name was and you said you didn't know."

"I don't know my name. Don't know what else to tell you."

"Nobody ever gave you a name?" Gerti asked.

"I guess. I don't remember if anybody gave me a name," she said.

"Sarah." Clements said from the front of the room, "You strike me as a Sarah."

"Eh, I don't know," she said, "You strike me as a Benitez."

Clements laughed and kept looking through the students' bags.

"Kaitlyn. Shannon. Agatha. Nancy. Sharon?" he rattled off the names one after another.

She smiled but shook her head.

"Ruth. Naomi. Esther." Gerti said.

"Biblical? Nice." Clements said.

"None of those sound right though," the girl said.

"What would you want your name to be?" Gerti asked.

"I like Naomi, or Agatha. I'd been thinking about Agnes. But I think I'd feel weird not knowing what my name actually was," she said.

"Gwen - Girl without name." Clements said, like he had won.

"Mmm, too quirky," she said.

Clements held up an old gray pen he had found in the desk.

"Lantus?" he said, reading off the old pen.

"That's kind of cool, but not me either," she said.

Clements dropped the pen back into the desk drawer.

"So what do you remember?" Gerti asked, settling into one of the plastic classroom chairs.

"I remember that I lived on the East Coast when I was younger," she said.

"Wow - how'd you get here?" Clements asked.

"Walked mostly," she answered with a grin.

"Where are you going?" Gerti asked, she couldn't imagine walking that far for nothing.

"I don't know guys," she said, starting to get frustrated. "There was something there I didn't want to be around and so I left. And before either of you ask, I don't remember what it was either. I'm just trying to get as far away from it as possible," she said.

"Hey, sorry," Clements said.

"Yeah, I didn't mean to pry," Gerti said, "I was just curious."

"No. I'm sorry. I'm just tired and my leg hurts like hell," she said, "It's also just frustrating. I feel like I should be able to remember but everything's just out of reach. It's like my brain is constantly on the edge of remembering."

"That's... rough." Gerti said.

"Wait, are you wearing pants?" the girl asked.

"No?" Gerti said.

The girl laughed.

"What? They're wet - I'm drying them. Have you ever slept in wet clothes? It's awful." Gerti said.

"That's fair." Clements said. He started undoing his pants.

"Whoa," the girl said.

"Calm down. She's right." Clements said. He clicked the button on the flashlight a few times and the light got dimmer each time. Then he turned it to face the far wall.

"What about you, Gerti, what's your deal?" Clements asked.

"What, specifically, do you want to know?" she asked.

"Well, I know you're from Waco and that you're working for the Bear Council," he responded, gesturing towards their signature shirt she was draping over a chair to dry. How long've you been working for them?"

"Only a few years," she said, "Before that though, I helped my Dad at his clinic. I was either doing that or hunting with my Mother."

"Right, you mentioned helping your folks." Clements said through a yawn.

The girl hooked her thumbs in her belt loops, hopped up, and pulled her pants off before throwing them onto a table. They made a wet slapping sound as they pasted themselves to the table's surface.

"I need to sleep," the girl declared.

They all agreed. Each of them rifled around finding backpacks to use as pillows and getting situated before trying to fall asleep under their jackets. The sound of the outside storm filled the room.

Chapter Five
September 22nd, 2114
College Station, Texas
Joseph Marion

There was a massively wide circular tower that had toppled to the ground at some point in the last century. It had fallen north towards the street from where Joe was approaching. A large section of it was scattered across a street that headed into the middle of campus. Its top had crashed into a large stone and glass structure. He carefully navigated around it and headed towards a building with a large dome on it. He passed several buildings that looked like they were about to crumble and skirted the edge of a long and short building.

Joseph heard several Trustee Bots come around the building's far corner. He froze - straining to see which direction they would head. They turned and started walking towards him. He slipped into a door that was a few feet away from him and clicked on his flashlight.

The walls of the room were charred and there were singed tables sitting around. The ceiling tiles were falling out and all the light fixtures were hanging loose - the plastic melted and drooping. On the far left wall was a garage door - in the middle of the room sat a car that actually looked like it was in pretty good condition. The tires were melted and flat, the interior of melted polyester, and the dashboard was cracked and melted. But it hadn't been exposed to the elements since before the fires.

'I bet this bad girl'd still drive if someone'd get a new battery for her,' he thought.

It was a Diurnal car - the same company that made most of the personal shelters that you could find. These ran entirely off their batteries. They were hard to find, but if you knew what you were doing, you could use Treighl batteries. If you had a dead Diurnal battery, you could even get it started with salt water. You had to leave the battery soaking for several days, but hey, that wasn't a bad tradeoff.

He looked around the room to see what else he could find.

'Might as well - while I'm here,' he thought. He also wasn't too eager to get back out there with the death robots.

The other rooms had fabrication machinery in them. The glass windows between the hallways and these rooms were all completely gone. The machines were melted or had been severely damaged by the fires. There were a few machines the size of tables that had long gantry rails and there were smaller machines that appeared to be more traditional mills and lathes.

Joseph was sad these machines were in such poor shape. They would have been a nice secondary prize to take back home. He briefly envisioned Bryan turning into an industrial hub. He smiled at the thought.

He moved south into the building until he found a door he could peek out of. There was a small alley and then another building. He didn't really know where he was going. He just wanted to find where the Trustee Bots were charging so he could nab their solar cells. He figured any tall building would let him watch them come and go.

Joseph crossed the alleyway and entered the next building. Getting to the south side was fairly easy. This building was mostly empty - only scorched remnants of the pre-fire world remained. Left behind like a snapshot that had been mummified.

He looked out a door and saw a street and a large open courtyard. On the other side of the courtyard was a tall square building with tall columns along the outside perimeter. He watched the open area for movement. After a few minutes of stillness, he opened the door and moved across it. He passed a crumbling building to his right and approached the towering building with columns.

Once inside, he found stairs and began climbing. The inside of the building seemed to be old offices. Thin partitions were burnt away and melted computers sat on top of burned desks. He reached the top of the building and was taken aback by how much stronger the wind and rain felt this high up. He cursed. He didn't want to go out close enough to the edge as he would need to for a closer look.

Realizing his short sightedness, he simply went to the bottom of the stairs, exited the stairwell, and looked around the top floor of the building. He found an office and looked out that window.

'I swear, sometimes I think Steven was right about me,' he thought. Steven was Joseph's older brother who had always called him stupid. *'But in that older brother's endearing kind of way,'* he thought.

Steven had been killed in that shootout all those years ago. His older brother had always been preternaturally good at fixing things and Joseph had always been envious of him for it.

He had fixed the family's radio when it short circuited and he must have fixed half the town's cars for Frank. Joseph was pretty sure that's why Frank was able to win his first election at all. He taught Allen most of what he knew about repair and most of what Joseph knew came from watching his brother while he was working.

Joseph wiped tears from his eyes and kept looking around the campus. There was a large building to his left but it wasn't very tall. There was a huge courtyard in front of him and a large building to his right that had a dome in the center of its roof. Joseph couldn't quite tell for sure but it looked like there was also a large antenna standing next to the dome.

A sudden light drew his eyes towards the bottom of the building with the dome. It looked like someone was shining a flashlight at a door. The light was there for a second then turned off. Joseph looked around for the source of the light but nothing stood out. Then, two figures started moving from the building to his left. One normal sized person and a larger one to their right. It was either a larger creature or two people moving really close to each other. Joseph strained his eyes trying to make out the details.

The figures moved towards the door, where the light had been shining, and entered the building. *'Interesting,'* he thought. He decided this was a good place to watch the Trustee Bots. It was mostly dry, the building seemed as sturdy as could be expected, and it gave him a good view of the campus. Maybe ten minutes went by, and a light came on inside one of the fourth-floor rooms of the domed facility. It wasn't a lightbulb but maybe a flashlight. A couple minutes and the light became much dimmer before turning off completely. Joseph stayed in this room for a couple hours just watching the Trustee Bots coming and going.

The rain got stronger and died down a few times but it never stopped. He did notice a lot of the Trustee Bots walking to the front of the domed building before coming back. Well, he couldn't tell if they were the same one or different ones. Maybe they were going to a charging station or maybe they were going along an assigned patrol path.

Either way, Joseph wanted to get a better look at the front of the building. He decided he would go into the large domed structure. He'd enter the door he knew was open but he'd stay on the south side of the building away from the room with the light.

He carefully made his way down the old stairwell and found a door that opened out into the courtyard. He waited for a patrol of Trustee Bots to pass by before he slowly opened the door and crossed the courtyard. The door the group went through was still unlocked. He slipped inside and shined his flashlight into the large room. It was dark enough he was willing to hazard the light, even with the people upstairs. The beam glinted off an old bronze bell that was lodged into the tile floor in the center. An array of regal columns encircled the room. There was a staircase in the central room but it was crumbled and filled with large chunks of concrete and debris from the ceiling. He quickly and quietly went south down a hallway being mindful of stepping around debris. The last thing he wanted was to alert whoever was upstairs.

He walked with his flashlight and pistol out. He looked for a stairwell on the south side of the complex but wasn't able to find one. Joseph circled back to the north side of the building and found a staircase there. He cursed to himself.

He holstered his gun and used his free hand to cover the head of the flashlight so that only a few beams of light passed through. He carefully walked up the steps until he reached the fourth, and top, floor. He stepped out into a hallway. There were rows of doors on each side. About half of them were closed. He tried to keep the sparse beams of light from hitting the bottom of the doors - to keep light from going under them. He heard talking from behind one of the doors.

He stopped, turned off his flashlight completely, and listened.

"I don' know," said a woman's voice, quietly.

Joseph put his ear against the door, trying to hear better. Light snoring came from the room. These people could be anyone.

"I just don't get it," a small girl's voice said. It was hoarse. "He was a student."

"Well, they're not running the way they're supposed to," the first voice said.

85

"Yeah, but this had to have been just before the fires - from what they were saying. They should have been working," the hoarse voice said.

"I don' know, Gwen," the other voice said.

"Yeah, I'm still not on board for that one." Gwen said, chuckling quietly.

"Well, we know that he and his professor were bein' watched. Maybe they crossed someone they shouldn't've," said the second voice.

"Maybe." Gwen said, "I really want to find out."

"We'll look around for a little tomorrow," said the first voice.

"Thanks." Gwen said, "And hey Gerti, thanks for earlier."

"'Course."

Joseph listened for a minute longer but the two girls seemed to be done talking for the night. He lightly pushed off the wall and regained his footing. He slowly backed away and covered the flashlight before turning it on.

Joseph walked aways down the hall before noticing a door that looked freshly tampered with. He shined the flashlight inside and saw an ancient corpse curled up in a supply closet. The body had a Treighl Trooper MK III laying curled up under its long-decayed arm. Joseph felt a pang of sorrow at the sight. He had seen more common models these used by some guards at the Diurnal shelter as attack dogs - mostly mark II's.

Apparently some people kept them as pets before the world ended.

He moved his attention to the rest of the small room. There was a ladder in the closet that led to the ceiling. He bet that it led to the roof. Joseph carefully climbed past the corpse, and his faithful guard dog, to grab the ladder. The hatch on the ceiling did open onto the roof.

The rain whipped at him as he stepped onto the rain slicked surface. Joseph shined the light around and saw a small temporary building at the base of the antenna. It was, maybe, ten by ten and made of cemented cinder blocks. A thick harness of cables ran out of a sealed hole in the side and led to the front of the building. The massive green dome loomed behind him.

Joseph walked over to the edge of the roof and knelt down to keep from being pushed off by the winds. They tried their best. The thick harness of cables ran all the way to a building in the middle of the courtyard. That building looked like it was probably built in a factory and set in place. The walls were stamped metal and had "Trustee" embossed on the side. It was about twenty by forty feet.

A door on the fabricated structure swung out in response to two Trustee Bots approaching. They stepped inside and the door closed. Seconds later, another door opened and two more Trustee Bots walked out to start their patrols. They each paused for a moment and gave a solemn salute to a brass statue that stood in front of the building Joseph was on.

"Well, damn." Joseph muttered to himself. He carefully turned away from the edge and went over to the building under the antenna. There was a keypad to the right of the door with a covered screen. He lifted the cover. *"Please provide a valid tech ID card or enter passcode."* Joseph keyed in 1234. It was worth a shot. The screen flashed red and said *"Denied."* He looked at the harness and thought about just hacking through it. He decided not to since it was raining and he had no idea what kind of voltage or amperage was running through it.

Somewhat defeated, he returned to the hatch and climbed down the ladder.

"Smaller goals," he thought.

Joseph picked up the mechanical dog - it weighed about twenty pounds - and moved it to a classroom on the far end of the hall from the other people. He carefully set it down on a desk and looked it over. He noted the changes to the MK.III on either side, and he also noticed all the screws on the outside case were stripped. He had seen that on a lot of devices. It was usually because someone was taking the screw out, and putting it back in more than was intended. No problem though.

Joseph pulled out his bit set and looked through for the right ones. The screws looked like they were originally hex heads that had been partially rounded out on the inside. He tried his hex heads but none of them fit quite right.

Joseph sighed to himself.

He hated doing this but he looked through his star bits until he found one that would work. Joseph took the gun oil out of his bag and put a drop on top of each screw so that the oil would fall into the threads. Then, he slid the screwdriver into the stripped screw, applied downward pressure, and slowly rotated it. The rust on the bolt broke and it started spinning freely. He did that to four more screws and the service panel popped off. Most of the time that didn't work completely but he was happy this time was an exception.

The panel on the inside had a small digital readout and a few buttons. He pressed the button that said service. The little readout displayed "*LoBt.*"

"I bet, buddy. We'll have to take care of that later, though," he said quietly.

He put a few drops of his gun oil on each joint and slowly worked them back and forth until they could move somewhat freely. It took him about thirty minutes to do that with all of them. He looked at his watch. 12:05am.

He yawned and then remembered he had a gun that would likely be rusted solid by the morning if he didn't clean it. He laid his pistol out on a table and disassembled it. He wiped down each part with his shirt before carefully placing a few drops of oil in the trigger group, slide, and slide rails. He assembled it and quietly racked the slide a few times before putting a round back in, closing the slide, and loading a magazine. Seven rounds in the magazine plus one in the chamber - just like Steven had taught him.

Joseph yawned hard enough that his jaw hurt. He moved a few chairs in front of the door and then found a place on the opposite wall to lay down. He was wet, cold, and miserable but he did eventually fall asleep.

A woman's scream shattered Joseph's sleep. He jolted up, felt around for his flashlight and clicked it on. He grabbed his pistol and listened. The screams didn't stop. The person screaming would take breaks to breathe but they kept screaming. The person screaming yelled something but Joseph couldn't tell what it was. It sounded like it was Gwen - the girl with the hoarse voice. He pulled the chairs away from the door and ran down the hallway.

"Holy shit! It's so hot!" she yelled.

"It's gonna be okay," a man's voice said.

The girl kept screaming still.

Joseph didn't really know what to do. He wanted to help them but how do you start that conversation?

"Do y'all need help?" he asked through the door. To his horror, he had holstered his pistol and knocked on the door. The screaming turned into muffled grunts of pain.

They didn't answer.

The door bolted inward and revealed a girl standing on the other side of a table. She was aiming a rifle at Joseph's chest. She was wearing a green flannel shirt and no pants. Joseph would've laughed if she also wasn't holding him at gunpoint.

"Whoa! I just heard screaming!" He slammed himself against the hallway wall to the right of the open door. He realized that the rifle's round could still completely ruin his day through the wall but he felt slightly better. "I just heard screaming and I wanted to help!" he yelled.

"Who are you?" the man asked.

"My name's Joseph, I'm from Bryan."

"Why are you here?" the rifle girl, Gerti, asked. Joseph assumed that was Gerti anyway, process of elimination and all that.

"Ju...st let him in. Shit!" Gwen said through gritted teeth.

"May I?" Joseph asked.

"Yeah, do anything and I'll put a hole through you," she said.

"Yes ma'am - totally fair," he said, before peeking his head into the room.

She was still holding the rifle, but it was at the ready and not aimed at his torso. The man was kneeling down next to a young woman who was laying on the ground under a rain jacket. Her leg had been pulled on top of the jacket and he was examining it with a bright flashlight. He was having trouble maneuvering the leg with one hand holding the flashlight.

"Here." Joseph said, holding out his hand to take the flashlight. The man's hair was almost completely shaved. His face was thin and jagged. He was definitely one of the cadets. The cadet handed Joseph his flashlight.

"Thanks," the cadet said.

Closer now, Joseph could get a good look at the girl's leg. There was a massive crater wound that ran through her calf. There were bandages, Joseph figured the cadet had just cut off, laying under her leg. The skin around the injury was dark red and inflamed. The crater wound had yellowish white foam seeping out from behind strands of tissue that connected one end to the other. The cadet apologized to the girl before scooping out handfuls of foam. She screamed anew.

"Where'd y'all get that medgel?" Joseph asked.

"Uh. One of the medic bots gave it to her," said the cadet.

"That makes sense. It does this when it's expired." Joseph said.

"Do you know how to fix it?" Gwen asked frantically.

"Yeah - he's doin' it," he answered, pointing at the cadet.

The cadet nodded and continued to pull the foam out.

Joseph turned to the girl with the rifle.

"Do you have any water?" he asked. "For the foam,"

She retrieved a metal canister from a bag on the ground. She unscrewed the large cap and handed it to him. Joseph waited for the cadet to get most of the foam out before pouring the water into the wound to flush out the rest.

"Was this a gunshot from earlier today?" Joseph asked.

"Yeah," the cadet said calmly. He was focused on the wound as he turned the girl's leg over and started scooping out foam.

"How'd you know?" Rifle Girl - Gerti asked.

"I didn't. I just heard gunshots earlier," he said.

She used her rifle as a staff to kneel down and look at the wound. Joseph realized that Rifle Girl, Cadet, and Gwen were all only wearing shirts and underwear. Their pants were hanging around the room.

"It wasn't me. It was one of the bots." Gerti said.

"I didn't think it was you. I heard energy guns before I heard gunfire. I figured y'all got in a fight with the Trustee Bots." Joseph said.

The area around the wound was covered in second degree burns but the tissue inside the wound had grown into the crater and was already scarring over.

"Is that better?" the cadet asked.

Gwen nodded her head. She relaxed and laid back down. Her face still showed signs of pain.

"Bryan has a few newer cans of medgel and a doctor. It's about an hour and half walk from here. I need to look into some stuff here but once I'm done I can take y'all back there." Joseph said.

"What are you looking for?" Gerti asked.

"The solar cells that recharge the Trustee Bots. We need them."

"Won't taking those kill the bots?" the cadet asked.

"Would that be a bad thing?" Gerti asked in reply.

"They protect the campus. They protect us," the cadet said, suddenly afraid.

Gerti looked at the cadet then pointedly looked down at Gwen's leg.

"Okay yeah, they protect us if we follow the rules. There have been a lot of people trying to get in here, over the years, and the bots have always stopped them." the cadet said.

"From what I've read, solar cells lose most of their effectiveness after about ten years." Joseph said. "I'm sure the fires sped that process up by a lot. If they've been working for the last century, that probably means they have a system of repairing or replacing the cells. I'll try not to disable all of them but I do need a few of them."

The cadet twisted his face.

"I promise." Joseph added.

"Okay, but I'm coming with you," he said.

"No. You need to stay here with her. I'll go with him." Gerti said.

Joseph thought about jumping in to say 'that's okay with me' but his Mom had always told him 'never interrupt a conversation that's goin' your way.'

"But -" the cadet started

"Benitez, just shoot him later if he kills the bots." Gwen said.

Benitez, the cadet, closed his eyes and rubbed his forehead.

"Fine," he said finally.

Gerti got dressed and checked her rifle over. She frowned when she pulled the bolt back and looked in the chamber.

"What's up?" Joseph asked.

"I haven't cleaned my rifle. There're already patches of rust."

"I have some oil - if you want."

"You wouldn't mind?"

"'Course not. It'd be a shame to let a piece like that rust over." Joseph led her to the room he had been sleeping in. "Honestly, I'm surprised that gun still works. It was old before the fires," he said, over his shoulder.

"You know it?" she asked.

"Yeah, it's a mosin. Seven six-two by fifty-nine - no, fifty-four."

"The girl recognized it too but I've never seen one. Other than mine."

"They're rare these days. I shouldn't be surprised it's lasted though - Russians built things to last."

"Russians? Are they from the east coast?" she asked.

"Why?" he asked, chuckling.

"That's where the girl's from."

"Ah. No. Russia is across the Atlantic Ocean - way past the east coast."

"How'd my Mom get it then?"

"Maybe a collector from before the fires?" he said, with a shrug. Joseph found the oil and gave it to her. While she was disassembling and cleaning her rifle, Joseph fiddled with the Trooper. The legs were still stiff but they could move.

"Careful with that. It tried to bite me earlier," she said.

"Really?"

"Yeah, I think it belonged to the guy in the closet."

"That makes sense. Damn, that's sad. It must have run its battery dry watching over him."

"It's just a bot," she said.

"Trooper models are different though. People used to keep them as pets and their programming was to protect their owner at all costs. I saw a trooper self-destruct to destroy a raider's truck. Saved the whole caravan. I'm gonna try to fix this one - I think it just needs a new battery - Maybe a wire brush to its joints. Wait, why were you messing with the corpse?" he asked, looking up at her.

"David Liebowitz. He was an engineering student here before the fires. I was hired to find something he was working on."

"By the Bear Council?"

"Yeah."

"Did you find what you were looking for?" he asked.

"I think so," she said, "Do you have a plan to get past the bots at the charging station?"

"No, I wish I could get into the control room. I bet we could disable them from there but it's locked - says it needs a valid tech ID."

"Like this?" Gerti asked, holding up a white plastic ID.

Joseph looked at it closer.

"Hot damn, yeah, maybe," he said grinning.

Chapter Six
September 22nd, 2114
College Station, Texas
Joseph Marion

"Are you going to disable them?" Gerti asked.

Joseph walked to the door of the classroom and poked his head out into the hall to make sure no one was listening before returning to Gerti.

"If I can. Do you know how many people these bots have killed?" he asked.

"No."

"They don't always stay on campus. They have patrols that go out into the old city and make sure people are following the same rules as here. They attack caravans for travelling without vector IDs - whatever the hell those are - they terrorize anybody who doesn't live behind a wall. Even then, they've killed guards on our walls for being armed - which was apparently against the law at the time. They're a menace. It's like saying you're protected because you live in a prison guarded by tigers."

"And the tigers have guns." Gerti said thoughtfully.

"And the tigers have guns," he repeated, laughing quietly.

Gerti slid the bolt of her rifle into place and threw the gun over her shoulder.

"Alright, where's the control room?" she asked.

"On the roof. There's a ladder in the closet." Joseph said with a smile. He appreciated the furrowed brow of new determination on her face.

The rain and wind had almost completely died down. The screen on the keypad lit up green when Joseph held the ID card up.

"Beautiful," he said under his breath.

The door made a clunking noise and unlocked. They stepped into a small room with a desk wrapping around three of the walls. There were computer monitors lining the desk and several chairs. Piles of trash littered the floor. It had been a messy workplace.

Joseph peeked his head under the table and looked at the computer towers. The fans were locked in place by a century of dust. The towers were putting off a lot of heat. He stuck his finger through the fan cover and tried to spin it - it moved but only a little.

He scanned the room with his flashlight. There was a Treighl battery sitting on the desk on the far wall. It had one metal terminal at the top that would plug into whatever needed power. Joseph didn't really understand how that worked though. His experience with normal batteries was that they needed two terminals - a positive and a negative - but whatever, the Treighl engineers had their own magic. He also knew that you couldn't test it with a multimeter.

The monitor behind the battery had a yellow light on the bottom right-hand side. The rest were completely off. He moved the mouse and the monitor blinked to life. There was a running list of model numbers and unit IDs. All the Trustee Bots laid out in a neat list. Most of them were red - marked as deactivated - but there were an alarming amount that were still green. Eight of the ID tags were yellow - listed as charging in the Academic Plaza Charging Bay. He double clicked on one of the green names and an options menu popped up.

- Activate
- Deactivate
- Return to zero
- Report to >
- Patrol Pattern >
- Mode >

He clicked on Mode >. Another dropdown menu loaded.

- Follow
- Assault

- Guard Area X
- Guard ID
- Passive
- Aggressive X

He highlighted all eight yellow tags and told them to "Report to > Academic Plaza. A loading icon twirled and then a confirmation light blinked. Their status bars said 'idle.' He clicked 'deactivate' and waited for the confirmation light. He checked the rest of the ID tags to make sure none of them said anything about returning to the charging station or Academic Plaza. None did. He highlighted all of the units and double clicked. It brought up the menu but there was a new option - upload software. He exited out and looked on the desktop for a software file. Clear as day - Version 2.15.

He double clicked it and it opened in Nova Sortum, the editing software designed for Amara+. The familiar, yet unknown, coding language loaded before him. It was all there. Might as well have been Greek for all he could do with it. He closed out of it and went back to the Unit control panel. He highlighted all the units again and selected Patrol Pattern > and deselected all the areas outside of the campus. Then he selected Guard ID and selected all the available options - selecting AM and PM. Then he selected the eight yellow unit tags and made them guard the ID of David Leibowitz, set them to follow, and made them passive.

"Do you see a flash drive around here anywhere?" he asked Gerti.

"A what?"

"Uh, don't worry about it." He pulled a desktop out from under the desk and opened the case. He pulled the drive out and dusted it off. Then he opened the computer he was working on and plugged it into an empty spot. After the computer recognized the drive, he transferred whatever he could. The running software, the software version, and any firmware updates he could find. After all that was transferred, he unplugged the hard drive.

There was shuffling behind him. He turned around to see Gerti idly shuffling stuff around on the desk.

"Sorry," he said, knowing she must be bored.

"No, take your time."

"I'm almost done anyway. We just need to go down to the charging station and check for charging cells." He explained the changes he had made to the Trustee Bots.

"So you can kind of keep your promise," she said.

"Well, so he can keep his tiger wardens as long as they stay within the prison walls." He smiled, slipped the hard drive into his bag, and grabbed the computer case he had gotten it from.

"Will you carry this?" he asked, indicating the battery. "Be careful not to touch the metal stud on the top."

She nodded and picked it up and cradled it in her arms.

He put the computer tower under his coat and they made their way out of the control room. They dropped the computer and the battery off in the room with the Trooper before heading to the room with Benitez and Gwen.

"It's us." Gerti said.

"Come in." Benitez said.

They entered the room.

"We set the Trustee Bots to not attack students and faculty at night. So y'all can walk around without worrying about getting shot. We also set them to not go outside the campus. So we can stop worrying about them killing us out there." Joseph said.

"*We's* generous." Gerti added.

"Thanks." Benitez said.

"No problem, Benitez." Joseph said.

Gwen chuckled through a cough.

"It's Clements," he explained. "My name's Clements."

"Why'd she call you -" Joseph started.

"Don't worry about it - just a joke. Let's finish this so we can get her to Bryan." Gerti said tiredly. They stepped out into the hallway.

"I have an idea - before we head outside," Joseph said. He ran into the room and quickly replaced the battery in the Trooper unit. Its lights came to life and it jumped to an attack position. Vents on the top of the unit opened as it hunched over growling at Joseph. He held up David's ID. The bot scanned it and looked at Joseph. It tilted its head for a second before jumping off the table and running down the hall. Joseph and Gerti followed. The bot had run into the closet and was sniffing around David's corpse making whining noises.

"Sheesh." Gerti muttered.

"Yeah..." Joseph breathed.

The bot looked back and forth between the corpse and the ID in Joseph's hand.

"You're gonna be okay." Joseph said, bending over to pet the bot. It snapped at his hand. "Okay. Take your time. We're gonna go out front if you need us." Joseph said to it.

Joseph and Gerti poked their heads into the classroom, to tell the others about the bot, before heading downstairs.

"The AI units in Trooper models were made to mimic real animals. They're the closest thing we ever got to true artificial intelligence." Joseph said. "Poor guy."

They stepped out the front doors and saw the eight bots that Joseph had set to follow David. He approached one and held up the ID. They scanned it and all started lining up behind Joseph.

"Nice." Gerti said, grinning and patted a robot on the plastic casing.

Joseph shined his flashlight into the charging station. There were eight bays, behind upswinging doors, that had space for the units to stay in.

"Hey, this's the one that saved the girl." Gerti said, patting a white medic unit on the torso. *"Treighl Robotics MU-1274"* written on the side. The unit's torso had breasts molded into the case and a more feminine face than the other units Joseph had seen.

'*Kinda weird,*' he thought.

"Can you imagine if we got her some new medgel?" Joseph asked. "It'd be a good asset for a town to have."

He scanned the charging station until he found the battery bank. Thankfully, the charging station seemed to have been two units sitting next to each other instead of a single unit. He found an internal switch and turned one of the sides off. Then, he unplugged the battery harness and slung it over one of the Trustee Bot's backs.

"Help me load these up," he said.

The two of them loaded sixteen batteries, the size of small shoeboxes, onto the Trustee Bots' backs. Then, Joseph climbed on top of the charging unit and pulled the four solar cells off. To his surprise, the plastic on the solar cells was almost completely melted away and covered in muddy dirt. One of the solar cells fell off and revealed two dark circles surrounded in weird symbols. Joseph would have called them runes in any other context. He'd have to investigate that later - for the time being, he handed them down to Gerti and she loaded them onto a Trustee Bot's back.

"I haven't gotten your name," he said, wanting to legitimize the knowledge he had gotten from eavesdropping.

"Gertrude Alverez. But I go by Gerti."

"Well, nice to meet you. What's the other girl's name?"

"I don't know," she said, tilting her head slightly.

"Wait, really?" he asked as climbed down off the charging station.

"Yeah, she doesn't know it either - Can't remember apparently."

"That's weird. What do y'all call her?"

"We don't, really. We ran through some names but she didn't like any of them."

"She strikes me as a Naomi," he said, hoping that wouldn't tip her off his overhearing.

"That's actually what I said. Clements pitched Gwen and Lantus but those were a no-go."

"Do you know how she ended up with all those scars?"

"No, I have no idea. It's a shame too. She's cute as a bug otherwise," she said.

"I haven't heard anybody say that in a while," he laughed.

"Oh, you know, just something my folks used to say.

"Same, actually. Do you think we should head back now or in the morning?"

"I would say now, for Naomi's sake. But it's your town. What do you think?" she asked.

"I think night would be better. That way there are less people to get frantic about strangers." he said.

"Sounds like a plan. I'll go get Lantus and Benitez," she said grinning as she jogged off to the Academic building.

"Hey! Want a light?" he called after her.

Gerti turned around and jogged back.

Joseph dug out the headlamp and pulled it on over his head before handing the flashlight to Gerti.

"Thanks," she said, before running off again.

Joseph casually scanned the plaza as he waited. There was a pole in the courtyard a little ways away from the charging station. There was a pile of what looked like debris sitting underneath it. It looked too orderly to be trash though. He started to go look but decided against it. A couple minutes passed and Gerti came back outside with the girl.

"Help me get her up." Gerti said.

Joseph and Gerti lifted the girl up onto the back of one of the Trustee Bots. She sat astride it.

"I'm gonna have to go back and get the other stuff." Gerti said.

"Don't worry about it, I'll go get them." The bots started to follow Joseph as he walked away. "Stay here with them," he said, pointing to Gerti and the girl.

They stopped walking and formed a circle around Gerti and the bot carrying the girl.

'Sweet,' he thought. He ran back into the building and up the stairs. The dog was still sniffing around the closet. "You comin' with us?" he asked.

The bot looked at Joseph for a moment before flopping down onto the ground next to the corpse and letting out a huff of air. "Buddy…" He started to pick the dog up but decided to leave it in the closet with its owner. "What's another century with a skeleton? Be safe, bud."

He pulled the closet door almost shut and went to the classroom. He grabbed the computer and ran back down to the plaza. "Clements took off?" he asked.

Gerti nodded.

"Alright, let's get going." Joseph started walking, watching the bots to make sure they followed him. Then a funny thought struck him.

"Walk twenty feet straight," he said to one of the bots.

It did so.

He climbed onto its back and told it to walk forward a hundred feet. It did and the rest of the bots followed in a straight line behind him. When he looked back to make sure, he saw Gerti climbing up onto one of them.

"Giddyup," he said to the bot. It didn't do anything. "Alright, take Old College to Downtown Bryan."

The bot started padding its way towards the road, took a right, then took a left a few minutes later. Joseph rested his hand on the grip of his pistol and chuckled at the mental image of tipping his hat to a car they passed. Something moved in the road, about a hundred feet in front of the Trustee Bot caravan. Joseph squinted to make out what it was. Two Trustee Bots were moving towards them. He started to yell back to Gerti and Gwen but didn't want to alert the bots to them. Instead, he clicked his headlamp on and shined them at the bots. Then he clicked it off and held out David's ID.

He looked back to see Gerti laying down flat on her bot - Gwen was already laying down as well. The two bots walked up and scanned David's ID before moving on past the caravan.

It only took an hour to get within sight of the wall before he told the lead bot to stop and wait. He led them to a brick building with thick glass tile windows that were still intact. Once they were inside, he told the Trustee Bots to wait. It was cramped but all eight bots fit into the room and went into sleep mode. He and Gerti helped the girl off the bot and supported her as they walked. Joseph clicked his headlamp on and checked his watch before they left the building. 3:54AM.

Seeing the time made his bones hurt.

He led them to the gap in the wall. He tried to see who was on watch but there wasn't a light on in the guard tower. He assumed there was somebody sitting in there and they had just turned the lights off to keep their night vision more intact. He kept looking and saw a pinprick of orange light from the end of a burning cigarette. Jordan. He led them through the hole in the wall behind the barbershop. A flashlight clicked on and spotlighted the three of them.

"Hands where I can - Joe?" Lucas lowered the flashlight. His voice was off kilter. He must've still been drunk from the party. Helluva time to take a patrol shift.

Joseph froze.

"Holy shit, did you actually go to the campus?" Lucas asked.

Joseph nodded slowly.

"Who are they?" Lucas asked, pointing to the girls.

"Gerti and Gwen. Gwen's hurt and needs medgel - Lucas, please don't tell anyone."

"Still not -" Gwen started.

"Did you find the cells?" Lucas asked.

110

"Yeah, and I found a lot more than that." Joseph said.

"Damn Joe - I didn't see anything." Lucas clicked his flashlight off and started walking down the alley towards Main. Joseph noticed Lucas wasn't walking entirely straight.

They waited for a minute before getting on Main and walking towards Joseph's apartment. He fumbled around for a key and pushed the door open.

He was greeted with Purcevale's startled meow and a shotgun racking a round into the chamber.

"Who's there?" Gloria asked from the darkness.

"Easy. It's just me and some new folks." Joseph answered.

Gloria turned on an electric lantern that was sitting on a small coffee table in front of the couch. She was laying down on top of the blankets with her muddy boots still on. Her hair was a mess, her eyes were puffy, and there was something green caked on the front of her shirt.

"Rough party, kiddo?" Joseph chuckled as he and Gerti helped the girl into the apartment. Gerti set her down in the chair by Joseph's workstation.

"Hmm." Gloria grunted. "Lucas and Krystal got in a fight and she left yelling - Allen wanted to play drinking games to distract him." Gloria mumbled as she set the shotgun on the floor and laid back down.

"And you lost?" he asked her but she responded with soft snores.

He pulled one of the blankets over his vomitty friend.

"How's your leg feeling?" Gerti asked Gwen.

"Lightly roasted," she responded.

Gerti looked at Gwen expressionless.

"It's tender and still a little warm. I'll be fine until later. I think cleaning it out helped a lot," she said through a smile.

"Still hurts?" Gerti asked.

"No."

"Well, let me know if it gets too bad," Joe said. "Doc's used to getting woken up at all hours. Bathroom's there if y'all want to change into something dry. I would offer the couch but - " Joseph motioned towards Gloria. He handed them both towels and blankets. "Does this work for y'all - for the night?"

"This is a really nice place." Gwen said.

"Yeah, it's dry. I don't have to worry about tigers and the door has a lock. I've slept in a lot worse places." Gerti said.

"Thanks. Me and Gloria - Gloria and I - do repairs around town. The mayor pays us pretty well to keep stuff running. She has her own place - she's just watching my cat."

"Did the mayor send you to the university?" Gerti asked.

"Oh. No. I'm definitely the one that broke the solar array earlier today and I really needed to be the one that fixed it. Leaving at night is actually illegal - which I'm hoping they'll ignore since I brought back a small herd of neutered Trustee Bots - with their chargers and a bank of batteries."

"You said the bots come around from time to time. Why haven't y'all used the batteries from one of those?" Gerti asked.

"We tried. Treighl units do this neat little thing where they destroy all their secret tech when they get… forcefully decommissioned. We've never had a working unit to disassemble." Joseph smiled. Tomorrow was going to be a good day. Well, maybe the day after tomorrow - once he had gotten caught up on sleep.

"Gwen, whenever you wake up we'll go see the doctor. Okay?" Gerti said.

"Okay. Hey, I really appreciate all the help," she said, limping to the bathroom.

"'Course." Gerti and Joseph said at the same time.

The four of them woke up to knocking at the door. Joseph sleepily got up and looked through the peephole. It was Allen.

"Hey Joe. Just wanted to check in - see how you were feeling. Mrs. Laredo was asking about you at service," he called through the door.

Joseph opened it.

"Thanks for coming by, Allen. You want to come in?"

"It's okay. You feeling any better though?" Allen asked.

"I wasn't sick." Joseph stepped outside and closed the door. "I went to the university to-"

"You went, where? And Gloria -" Allen looked pissed.

"Yeah, she lied for me. She's a champ. Listen, I brought back a bunch of Trustee Bots and their charging units. We can completely change the setup of the town. Forget running a few light bulbs and a fridge, we could - "

"Joe, I would've gone with you."

"You didn't seem too keen on the idea - when I brought it up."

"Yeah, because it's dangerous - you could've died. One of the guards could've caught you and turned you in."

"You think Miguel or Willow were gonna throw me in jail?"

"Yes. Because that's what they get paid to do. But that's besides the point - what you did was reckless. Did anyone see you leaving or coming back?"

"Lucas saw us coming through the hole in the fence."

"Behind Harold's?"

Joseph nodded.

"I told Lucas to - Okay. Okay. Okay, I'll talk to Lucas and make sure he doesn't say anything. I might be able to get Frank to say he gave you permission to leave or something - what all did you find?" Allen asked.

Joseph rattled off the list of things but didn't tell him where they were hidden.

"Did you grab the converters?" Allen asked.

"I figured we could use a few from the Trustee Bots." Joseph said.

"Okay. Yeah, that should work. Just stay here until I can talk to Frank." Allen started to climb down the stairs.

"Well hey, I have someone in here that needs to see Harrison."

"Gloria'll be fine, she's just -"

"No. Well yeah, she'll be fine but there's a girl in here that used expired medgel."

Allen closed his eyes and took a deep breath.

"What?" he asked.

"There was a girl at the university. She caught a bolt to the leg. We cleared the foam out of the wound but she's still injured."

"'We.' You and the girl, or are there more people?" Allen asked.

"There was another girl with her - and a cadet but he stayed on campus."

"Okay, so you found Trustee Bots, Treighl batteries - the chargers, and two strays that you snuck in through the wall. Is that everything?"

"Should be."

"Have you ever used a medgel gun?" Allen asked.

"I've seen one used."

"It's okay - you've used a caulk gun and it's basically the same thing. I'll stop by Doc's and get one for you. He owes me."

"Thanks Allen."

"'Course. I'm glad you're safe." Allen turned and walked down the stairs. Joseph went back inside and told them what Allen was doing.

"Lucas was at the barber?" Gloria made a 'yeesh' face. "You probably saved Harold's life." She had been listening at the door.

"Your barber's name is Hairy?" Gwen asked, once Joseph was back in the room.

"It's Harold and he's very strict about it." Gloria answered.

"Our doc's name is Harry though - Harrison. What's going on with Lucas and Harold?" Joseph asked Gloria.

"Krystal went to him after the fight," she answered.

"Eeegh. That's tough." Joseph said. Gerti was up and looking out the front window that overlooked the street.

"Is there another way out of here?" she asked.

"There's a window in the bathroom that has a fire exit. You worried?" Joseph asked.

"Just coverin' my bases," she said.

A few minutes later, there was a knock at the door. Joseph looked through the peephole and saw Allen standing there with Frank next to him.

He opened the door and let them in.

Chapter Seven
September 23rd, 2114
Bryan, Texas
Girl

Her leg still hurt like hell but it was far from the worst thing she had experienced. Even when it was burning and still covered in the expired medgel - even while Clements was digging it out. She couldn't remember when it was she had felt pain that was worse but she could remember it happened.

The scar on her right palm was most readily visible to her so she often found herself absent mindedly fiddling with the puncture mark there. She traced it to a small oval shaped scar on her wrist then followed it up to another three of the same type.

Her whole body was covered in puncture marks, knife cuts, scarified symbols, and several bullet wounds. She had no idea where they came from but she was always hurt when she thought about them.

Physically - yes, sometimes - the scar tissue on the larger ones never fully went away and the feeling was still dulled. But it was deeper than that for her. Like they shouldn't have been there or they weren't deserved. The person who put them there shouldn't have been able to. She had a hard time sorting out these ideas.

Usually when she got to this point she would hum a tune to distract herself but she didn't want to with all these people around her. Not that she should complain - she was happy to have company.

Gloria and Joseph were talking about some drama that was going on in the town and that was fun. Fun probably wasn't the most appropriate word for it but it was interesting to listen to.

Bryan seemed like a nice town from what she had seen. They collected rain water, had electricity, homes, families, and they would take in strangers. It felt like a real community. They had a wall and a town guard - they seemed fairly put together.

Before going to the university, she had stayed with the people living in some old Fairegrounds where they had built a castle wall out of stone. They were nice and enjoyed when she would sing for them but they were a little too spaced out for her. Before she left, they asked her where she was heading. She never had an answer for that question, so she just told them the first thing she thought they would enjoy. Which was "Continuing my journey." They nodded and wished her fortune before letting her out of their camp. They called her Calben, which they told her meant "person on a great journey" in an ancient language from one of their sacred texts.

Hairy's a pretty funny name for a barber - did he pick that job because of his name or did he even think about it until someone pointed it out? Did he pick the name? She needed to figure out what her name was. At least figure out what her name currently is.

Gerti asked something about exits. Gerti was late to the game - the girl had figured out where the exits were last night before laying down to go to sleep. She made sure the bathroom window was unlocked when she was in there changing and she had unlatched the front window lock as well. There was a knock at the front door. Joseph let two men in.

The younger one was taller and well-built with short, but shaggy, black hair. The other was thin and looked like he was in his mid-forties. They were both wearing clean jeans and buttoned shirts. The younger one was wearing a cowboy hat and had a pistol shaped bulge in his right pocket. She tried not to stare at his pocket for too long.

"Here's the medgel, Joe. Harrison still charged me twenty crystal. Guess my favor wasn't as valuable as I thought."

"I'll spot you the crystal." Joe laughed. The applicator was a matte gray cradle that held the medgel canister on top.

He walked over to the girl and lifted her leg onto a stool. The foam was cold as it filled both holes on her leg. An electric tingle ran through her body as it began its work. The medgel the bot had used was nothing like this.

"Hello ladies. I'm Frank Willard. I'm the mayor - welcome to Bryan. I heard you were injured helping Joe on campus?" the older man knelt down next to the girl.

"More or less. One of those bots shot me," she answered.

"They helped me get the parts back here." Joe said. He introduced Gertrude and her. Joe called her Gwen when he introduced her. It seemed she'd have to get used to getting called that for a while. It would pass eventually.

"Well, I'm glad y'all were there to get Joe back. Allen tells me you brought back quite the haul, Joe." Frank said.

"Yessir - I'm hoping we can get the power back up in the next few days." Joe said. The girl noticed Frank was avoiding eye contact with Joe. Instead he was moving from object to object in the small apartment - adjusting them slightly or lifting them to get a closer look.

"Let's hope you're right. I've agreed to say I sent you to the campus - if anybody asks. I don't appreciate that you broke curfew but I understand you did it for the town. I can only hope other people have the same dedication. Gloria, I still want to get in touch with your family for the wind generators. I think Allen's right - we need to diversify where our power is coming from. Joe, you're saying we can get power back, but from what Allen's saying, we'll be able to expand into a lot more with what you've found. If that's true, we'll have a party - maybe even make it a holiday if it works out the way he's hopin'."

"Joe was able to get that crane working with manual controls last year. I was thinking he would be able to rig up the bot's weapons as mounted guns around the town and we could use the bots as plow animals." Allen said.

"We could probably power a food replicator, if we could find one." Joe said.

"We could stop relying on the shelter." Gloria breathed.

Frank smiled. The smile had too many teeth. It sent shivers down the girl's spine. He turned to her.

"Will you be staying awhile?" he asked.

"I figure I'll have to. How long does the medgel take?"

"Usually a couple days - it depends on the wound." Allen answered.

"I hope you'll stay longer than that. I would ask you too -" Frank said to Gerti. "But I imagine, from the bear on your shirt, that someone's expecting you."

Gerti nodded.

Maybe the girl would go with Gerti if she'd wait to leave. Having someone to talk to on the road could be nice.

"Well, you and your bears are always welcome here," he said, while reverently holding up his right hand, making a claw.

Gerti returned the gesture.

"I'll probably head north as soon as I can get a good night's sleep," she said.

Frank nodded.

"I'll make sure to get you two somewhere comfortable to sleep. No offense Joe." Frank said.

"Place isn't really built for company." Joe said, looking around his little apartment.

"Gertrude, I have a favor to ask of you and Joe before you leave." Frank began. "Willow. C'mon in." Frank called out the open front door.

A younger woman with shoulder length white hair walked into the apartment. Her hair was truly white. Unnaturally white. Willow looked like someone you didn't want to mess with. She had an old H&K G3 slung across her chest in such a way that she could draw it quickly. She had a thick canvas belt that held several large magazines for her rifle.

The girl didn't like that Frank brought a gunman and kept her hidden like that. She understood but she didn't like it.

123

"Allen also said that y'all made contact with the cadets and that they were friendly?" Frank asked.

Joe was still kneeling by the girl, watching the foam as it began stitching her muscles back together. He turned to Frank and nodded.

"I want the two of you to go with Willow and make official contact with them. The campus clearly has untold potential we could use - or at least trade for."

"What about setting up the power?" Joe asked.

"Allen, Lucas, and Gloria will take care of it," he answered, waving off the question.

Gerti opened her mouth to say something but Frank cut her off.

"I'll pay both of you two hundred crystal. These kinds of relationships could help us grow the valley into more than just a collection of discordant groups. A community - a larger network of communities - working together to make something bigger."

The girl was taken aback. Two hundred blood crystals for a meet and greet with that group?

An average mutated person only held around twenty to twenty-two crystals worth of blood and that's if you were able to completely drain them. It took about a cup of blood to condense into a single crystal. Obviously, the crystals didn't have to come from a person. There were plenty of mutated animals that could supply that. Still though. Where the hell did he get that much? She thought about the two crystals in her pants pocket that came from her gunshot.

"I'll go. Gerti?" Joe asked.

She thought for a moment before shaking her head.

"That is a lot but I need to get back to the council." Gerti said, shaking her head.

"Did they give you a time frame?" Frank asked.

"No but -"

"Then there's no way for them to know you've already found whatever trinket they sent you out for. This won't take more than a few hours. We're lending Willow a truck to take y'all back to campus." Frank said, smiling.

Gerti thought a few more moments before agreeing.

"Perfect. If you're able, I'd like for y'all to leave as soon as possible." Frank said.

"The truck's out on the street if you want to get your shit together." Willow said, nodding towards the door.

"Willow, there's no need for the language." Frank said.

Joe and Gerti got dressed completely and got their gear together. They waved goodbye and went out the front door with Willow. Joe popped his head back in and asked Gloria to lock the place up.

"Allen, Gloria, do you mind giving me a moment with Gwen? If that's alright with you?" Frank asked.

The girl nodded.

Allen and Gloria stepped out the front door and pulled it to. Frank sat down on the couch and leaned forward towards the girl. Her stomach tightened.

"I know you don't trust me," he said.

"What?" she asked, surprised at his directness.

"I saw how you looked at me. I get it - it's okay. I admit, having Willow stay outside like that may seem, eh, shady, I guess you'd call it. She's just my personal guard and I didn't want to cause a panic in you or your friend. Does that put your mind at ease?"

"A little."

He smiled. There were still too many teeth. He smiled a little smaller - a little more genuine.

The girl locked eyes with the mayor - she didn't want to appear weak.

"Good. The last thing I want is for strangers to feel unwelcome. Do you have any other concerns I can address?" he asked.

"Two hundred crystals is a lot of money."

"Oh I know, but you have to pay well if you want good help. I know Joe and Willow are good help and I'm willing to bet good money that your friend is too. I would have asked you to go as well but I think your leg is in bad shape. Maybe you can sing down at the cafe. I

126

bet folks would enjoy that. I bet they'd pay to - if that was your concern."

"It wasn't really. How'd you know I sing?" she narrowed her eyes.

"You have a pretty voice. I just guessed that your singin' is pretty too. If pay wasn't your concern, what was?"

"A human, or I guess a human sized mutant, only gives twenty-ish crystals. Where do you get all your crystals from?"

"That's very specific," Frank chuckled. "But it's mostly from trading with various settlements. Why are you worried about it?"

"I've seen some groups keep - nevermind. I'm sorry for assuming..." she trailed off. She thought about a group she saw that had a mutated elephant lifted into a harness.

They kept it fed and bled it almost to death for its blood crystals.

Frank looked down at her scarred arms.

"It's okay. The world's a dark place and it looks like you've been out in it for a while."

She nodded - she had been. It'd be nice to stay for a while.

"I'll have Gloria and Allen take you to the cafe to get some food." He handed her a little green plastic circular token. "Give this to Mrs. Laredo and she'll fix you something up to eat. You're in for a treat actually - We have fried chicken on Sundays."

"Thank you," she said.

He nodded and stood up.

"I hope you consider sticking around for a bit longer," he said, before heading for the front door.

A couple seconds later, Gloria and Allen walked back into the apartment. They helped her get to the cafe just down the street. There was a brunette woman standing behind a small counter - maybe in her forties.

She, and everyone in the cafe, were wearing nice clothes. The men were wearing jeans and leather boots - the women were wearing dresses and wide hats. The girl had never seen people dressed this well. Most of the people were in the line approaching the woman and didn't pay the girl any attention. Allen and Gloria got in line with the girl and waited their turn for food.

"What'd Frank want to talk about?" Gloria asked. Before the girl could answer, the middle-aged woman behind the counter interrupted.

"Oh Honey," the woman said when she saw the girl's face. "What happened to you?" The girl started to respond when the woman shook her head and said "I'm sorry Sweetheart, that was rude of me. Do you want the chicken or the steak?"

"Uh, I don't know," she said. She didn't really know what either of those things were. How was she gonna choose. Everyone was looking at her.

"Get the chicken." Allen said.

"What's wrong with the steak?" the woman asked.

"Nothin' Ma'am, I just want her to try your chicken." The woman smiled, took their tokens, and gave them three plates of fried chicken. The girl looked at her plate as they walked to a vacant table. She didn't know what chicken was but she assumed, from the looks of it, that it was some kind of fried bread.

Chapter Eight
September 23rd, 2114
Bryan, Texas
Joseph Marion

"I ate during service." Willow said, handing Gerti and Joseph containers of fried chicken. She was maneuvering the truck through debris and burned out cars as she drove towards the university. The truck was a flat gray color and had an angular body that met at a peak in the middle of the frame. The interior had worn away decades ago and had been replaced with various types of fur stitched together.

"We used to have chicken in Waco but they all died out when I was little. How did y'all keep them alive?" Gerti asked.

"We didn't." Willow said. "We buy it from the shelter. It's not cheap, but the mayor wanted us to have it for Sunday lunches."

"Allen said it was around two crystal per pound. I've done the math, we have to be spending around three hundred crystal a week." Joseph said. Most things cost a couple crystals at most. A couple pounds of potatoes, a handful of common bullets, a new pair of pants - all cost a single crimson crystal. Two hundred for a quick meeting wasn't an offer Joseph would turn down - even if it was dangerous.

"Whatever it takes to keep getting elected - even if elections aren't until March." Willow said.

Joseph smiled thinking about the 'campaigns' they'd hold every year. They were mostly for show. Nobody really put in too strong of a fight against Frank.

"Two hundred crystal seems like a lot for this job." Gerti said.

"Yeah?" Willow asked.

"He has odd priorities. It's his money though." Joseph said, shrugging.

"Where does he get all the crystal though?" Gerti asked.

"Don't worry about it - trade mostly." Willow said.

"Who do y'all trade with? I haven't seen anybody up in Waco." Gerti said. Trade was scarce in this world. Most people didn't trust easily and were more likely to shoot on sight than anything else. Joseph was proud to live in one of the few towns where that wasn't the case.

"That's pretty far though. We trade with Delta and Anderson." Willow said, paying close attention to the torn road in front of her.

"How long have you worked for the mayor?" Gerti asked. Her eyes were locked on Willow in the rearview mirror. Joe wondered what she was looking for - she clearly didn't trust Willow.

"Since I turned eighteen. Sooo, five years. Seemed like a better gig than runnin' supplies or fixin' stuff. I worked security at the shelter before that though. What about you? How long've you been workin' for the Council?"

"Couple of years."

"How many of their crazy missions have they sent you on?" Joseph asked. He was turned in his seat looking at Gerti. He couldn't stop looking at her face. The way the light contoured around the scar that went across it. Realizing he was staring, looked elsewhere.

"This is my first one. They had me guardin' the clinic or hunting." Gerti said.

"Does it pay well? It's got to - how many we've seen come through here." Willow said, absentmindedly.

"What do you mean?" Gerti asked.

"We have bears come through here all the time."

"Really? I didn't know that." Gerti said.

"Yeah, about every other month we get one coming through town. Usually looking for the campus. 'Ve never seen one come back out though. I thought they would've told you that." Willow said, looking at Gerti through the rear-view mirror.

"No. They didn't. How many have you seen?"

"Ooooh, probably thirty. Somewhere in that ballpark." Willow said.

Gerti's jaw tensed - she glanced out the window at the passing buildings.

"What's wrong?" Joseph asked.

"I wouldn't've been able to find what I was lookin' for without Gwen's help. The same was true for everyone else they've sent here," she said.

"How's that?" Joseph asked.

"I can't read - nobody outside the council can. I wouldn't've been able to find what I was lookin' for without being able to read. Gwen was able to follow the clues to where David's body was. I never would've been able to find it. I would've been killed or've been forced to go back empty handed - and that's as good as getting killed."

"You think all those bears were sent to the campus? Why wouldn't they have sent someone who can read?" Joseph asked.

"The council citizens aren't allowed into the world," she answered, like that was self-evident and explained everything.

"Yeah but -" Joe started, before Willow cut him off.

"Alright, where are the cadets?" she asked, steering around another burnt out car.

They were pulling up to the end of Old College. Gerti guided Willow into the front of campus, through a large circular road, and up to a courtyard surrounded in archways.

There were four men in khaki uniforms standing in front of a door at the base of a four-story beige building. Each had a rifle slung over their shoulder. Joseph recognized them as garands - each with a stark white strap. They shielded their eyes from the harsh sun as they eyed the newcomer's angular metal truck.

"This is where I met them." Gerti said.

The three of them got out of the truck and approached the four men. Joseph raised an empty hand. The four men talked amongst themselves before one ran inside.

"You said they were friendly?" Willow asked quietly. She was holding her slung rifle at low ready. Clements came running out past the three men.

"Y'all need to leave! I'm lucky they didn't string me up for -" he started.

"Cadet Clements!" a booming voice called from the building. An older man with short gray hair stood at an open window on the fourth floor. "Get away from those thieves!"

Gerti and Willow both started backing up to the truck - Joseph did likewise.

"You, stay where you are!" the man shouted.

"We just came to talk!" Joseph called out.

The man mumbled something in response but none of them could hear what he had said.

"I'm coming down," he yelled, before disappearing from the window.

"What happened?" Gerti asked Clements.

"I told them about the Trustee Bots. I thought they'd be happy about the changes you made but they -"

"Clements! You heard him. Get away from them!" one of the cadets shouted.

Clements didn't immediately. The cadet raised his weapons - Willow snapped her rifle up in response.

"Easy, killer," she said.

Joseph heard two small clicks come from Willow's rifle - he knew that meant it was on automatic. She was prepping for a knock down drag out fight. Willow circled around behind the truck and rested her rifle on the hood.

Gerti got behind the cab.

Joseph stayed where he was and made sure his hand wasn't anywhere near his holstered pistol. His heart was pounding in his chest. Clements jogged back into the building and reappeared a moment later pleading with the older man.

The older man ignored Clements as he stepped into the harsh sunlight. He was now wearing a garrison cap that matched his uniform.

"Cadet Clements told us that you meddled with the Trustee Bots and that you stole half of their charging station. Is it true? I don't have any reason to doubt what he said."

"Yes. I took parts of the charging station. But-" Joseph said. He was holding his hands out - they were shaking. They all had a lot of guns pointed at them and it didn't seem like the situation was going to calm down.

"And you stole eight of the campus bots?"

"Yes."

"What could possibly make you come back after committing such a heinous violation?"

"We're from Bryan. Our mayor wanted us to make contact with you. So our groups could work together." Joseph said, motioning back to Willow.

"I'm not impressed with the character of Bryan that they would send you to steal from us. Not only did you steal from us, you stole Trustee Bots!" His index finger jutted towards them as he hurled accusations. "They are the only thing keeping us safe from the wastes. The penalty for this violation must be death!"

"That seems harsh. At least hear us out." Joseph said. He was regretting not taking cover.

"Commander, please." Clements pleaded.

"Your skill as our medic is the only thing keeping you from facing a firing squad. I will not put up with another word," his commander said, dismissively.

"We're going to get in the truck and leave." Willow called.

"You will face justi-"

"We're either leaving, or I'm blowing a hole in your chest." Gerti said.

There was movement in the building. A handful of cadets had appeared - all aiming rifles. Gerti's finger hovering over her trigger - sweat beaded on her forehead.

Everyone was still for a moment. The commander's face was beet red. Joe's heart was pounding in his chest as he took tentative steps back towards the truck.

"Kill them!" he yelled, spittle flying from his mouth.

Willow began firing as soon as she heard the K.

An explosion of automatic fire belched from her heavy rifle and toppled the three men by the door - the commander dove to the ground and Clements ducked down - bullets and screams flying over his head.

Gerti dropped one of the cadets in the windows. His body fell back out of sight.

Joseph clambered into the back of the truck and slammed the door shut - bullet holes pierced the truck's body and broke the window. He ducked as the shattered glass rained down on him. He drew his pistol and fired at the building through the now open window - fairly sure he had only damaged the brick facade. It had been a long time since he had fired his gun in anger.

Gerti and Willow jumped in the car and Willow gunned it out of the courtyard - bullets punched holes through the truck as they sped off.

One of the bullets punctured the tires and the car started driving with a heavy wobble.

Trustee Bot sirens started blaring throughout the campus. A hail of energy weapons started screaming towards the truck. The bolts melted away the body of the truck wherever they hit. One landed squarely, punching a hole in the hood.

"Road's blocked!" Willow yelled. She pulled a hard U-turn and started speeding away from a group of Trustee Bots. "Get low!" A couple rounds pounded against the left side of the truck as they passed the courtyard again.

"Are y'all good?" Willow asked as she swerved around a Trustee Bot that was charging its weapon.

"No blood here." Gerti said, patting herself down.

"S-same." Joseph said. He marveled at how far south this had gone.

A Trustee Bot stepped into the road causing Willow to take a hard turn. An energy bolt shot through the middle of the cab. Joseph looked through the new hole and fired at the bot. The pistol clicked empty.

Willow said something from the front but Joseph couldn't hear her through his ringing ears. She was looking back at him. There was a loud crash Joseph slammed into the seat in front of him as the car came to a sudden stop.

* * *

Brandon Clements laid prone on the concrete courtyard - Commander Rose was writhing on the ground next to him. Gunshots thundered from the dorm windows. A pool of blood started to spread from the commander's body - his uniform darkening around a large hole torn in his lower torso.

"Commander." Brandon breathed. "Help! I need help!" He rolled the commander over and tore at his shirt buttons.

A fount of blood came from his gut. Brandon cursed, pulled off his cap, and shoved it into the wound. "I need help!" he yelled again.

Ashlee Crowles, a new cadet, ran out to him.

"Put pressure right here," he ordered frantically.

She took his spot pressing down on the wound. Air escaped the commander's throat in a curse. That was good - it meant he was alive.

Brandon ran over to the three men laying on the ground. Thomas was struggling for breath - Forest and Grant were not. The front of Thomas' uniform was soaked to a deep maroon. He looked up at Brandon.

"How's it - look, Clemons?" Thomas mumbled through Brandon's name. He was in shock.

"I'll let you know." Brandon carefully unbuttoned Thomas's shirt and pulled up his undershirt. Three gunshot wounds across his chest were oozing thick rivers of blood. "You're gonna be okay, Tom." Brandon said, trying to muster reassurance. He put pressure on the wounds but he could feel the blood still escaping.

"Goo', maybe they'll make me - Lieutenant for this." Thomas said weakly. He was fading - not making any sense.

"Damnit. I need help!" Brandon's voice quivered as he screamed.

Two more gunshots came from the dorm as the truck passed back by the courtyard.

"Help!" Brandon yelled with all his being - his chest hurt from it but he didn't notice. He pulled his uniform shirt off and pressed it against the gunshots. They immediately wicked up Thomas' blood. He pressed and prayed.

"Clements," a soft voice said.

Brandon turned to see Dr. Grady struggling to kneel down. He was looking at Thomas' face - it was motionless.

Two cadets, it looked like Hughes and Jacob, ran over to Commander Rose with some old mops and a blanket. They made a stretcher and lifted the commander onto it. They hoisted him up and carried him inside.

"Come inside. You'll need to see this." Dr. Grady said as he turned to limp into the dorm.

Brandon tried to stand but he couldn't make his body obey. It had all happened so fast. He felt a hand on his shoulder - he looked up to see Ashlee.

She was holding his garrison cap out to him. He reached out to grab it and saw his hands covered in blood for the second time in a twenty-four-hour period. He took the cap and stood.

"Thanks," he muttered.

Heavy metal footsteps started clunking onto the courtyard.

"Please remain where you are. There appears to be an active shooter on campus."

A horde of Trustee Bots was descending on the battle scene. Ashlee and Brandon went into the dorm and locked the door behind them.

Dr. Grady and Commander Rose were in one of the interior dorm rooms. Hughes and Jacob were holding bright flashlights over the commander - who was laying on an empty bed.

"Point three milligrams of morphine." Grady calmly ordered Brandon. "Then help me get him turned over."

Brandon opened Grady's leather bag and did as he was told.

The commander's muscles relaxed. They turned him over and cut his uniform away. Brandon grimaced at the exit wound - It was a gaping crater of bloody meat barely covered with loose flaps of skin.

"Holy shit." Hughes breathed. "Is he gonna die?"

Grady scowled at the cadet.

Brandon grabbed a handful of clean rags and began pressing them into the wound. Together, they dabbed blood out of the mess. Grady carefully pressed a needle into the commander's arm and attached it to an IV bag of clear liquid that he hung on the bedpost.

"Hughes, I need you to go into my room and grab one of the medgel canisters - and the applicator." Grady said.

"We used the last one a couple weeks ago when Anders fell on the-"

"We haven't gotten more?" Grady asked.

"Nobody's been to the-"

"This man's going to die because y'all were too lazy to -" Grady took a deep breath. "Clements. Take the crystal in my bag and go get some. Quickly. Run."

"Y'sir," he dug around in the doctor's black shoulder bag and pulled out a canvas drawstring pouch.

The crystals clinked against each other as they moved inside the bag. Brandon checked his pockets to see what he had on him as he walked to the door. Just his ID and the small bag of crystal. He held up his ID and opened the door. One of the Trustee Bots scanned it.

"Are you injured, Mrs. Benitez?" it asked.

"No," he thought about telling the Trustee Bot about Commander Rose but he didn't want them to burst in and see all the cadets with rifles.

"Are these the assailants?" The bot pointed a decrepit hand at Thomas, Forest, and Grant - their rifles laying besides them.

"Yes." Clements said after a moment.

"Thank you. I'll notify authorities to come retrieve them. Is anyone else injured?

"No."

"Thank you, Mrs. Benitez."

"Thank you, Mrs. Benitez," said another.

"Thheeeeeee Mmmmmzzzzzz" squawked another.

They formed a circle around the fallen cadets and held their weapons at the ready. Their antennas came up and the light on top began blinking.

Brandon took off running for the health building. It was just to the east of Academic Plaza. He didn't like going there. He didn't like seeing all the memorials left at the flagpole over the many years. Still, he felt a need to see it from time to time.

He went a little further east towards a large open field and cut north. The flagpole was in the middle of the center walkway leading to the Academic building, a metal fasci sat at the bottom. It had a mountain of items around it - each represented a cadet that had died in the last century. A weathered brass statue of an old confederate general, Sul Ross, stood in silent vigil of the memorial.

The health building was on the far side of the Academic Plaza. He checked the plaza before crossing it and didn't see anyone. He didn't think the folks from Bryan would hurt him but he also didn't think they would've killed at least three of the cadets and potentially the commander.

Rose had told the cadets to kill them. If he lived, he would probably exile Brandon or have him killed.

There was a machine on the second story of the health building that would dispense medical equipment - including medgel. It was a large machine that took up most of an eight-foot-wide wall. There was a small door in the corner that led to a room behind the machine.

Brandon touched the small screen on the machine and it lit up. He scrolled the menus and selected medgel. It made a whirring noise and then an error message popped up on the screen. He had hoped it would have enough power, or whatever, to create the medgel without having to use the crystals.

He went through the door to the back and found the small compartment on the side of the machine. He dumped a small handful of crystal into the compartment and closed it. He figured it was probably a forty crystal - maybe more.

Brandon went around to the front and selected medgel again. It made a happy dinging noise and dispensed a can of medgel out into a receptacle on the bottom. He grabbed it and headed for the door. There was no point in checking the compartment for leftover crystal.

Whatever the machine did, it always consumed every bit you gave it.

Chapter Nine
September 23rd, 2114
University Campus, Texas
Joseph Marion

Joseph struggled to get out of the kickspace. His right arm was throbbing from where he had made contact with the back of the passenger seat. His head was spinning.

Gerti opened the door behind him and helped him out. Willow crawled over the center console and through the passenger door.

"Joe, where's the charging station?" Willow asked. Her eyes and her rifle searched the surrounding buildings for threats. Not surprisingly, she was calm - this was her element.

He looked around until he saw the building with the green dome. It was close.

"It's just past those two buildings. Why?" he asked.

"I'm gonna destroy it. Screw those guys." She grabbed her rifle and something else from the truck's dash compartment.

"I can just disable them." Joseph said. He really didn't want to make this situation worse.

"Will they be able to enable them again?" Willow asked, checking over the item she had pulled from the truck. It was a small pineapple grenade that was covered in a thin layer of rust.

"Maybe, but I don't think they know how."

"So, I'm gonna destroy the charging station - maybe the control center too." Willow said, tucking the grenade's spoon handle into her belt.

"Frank's paying us to make contact with the cadets so we can work together. Completely destroying their bots isn't going to make them want to work with us." Joseph said.

"They tried to kill us - they can eat a fat one. If we can't work together, Frank's gonna want us to make sure they can't work against us."

"What do you think, Gerti?" Joseph asked.

"Personally, I don't think y'all should fight the cadets. They seem like they stay on campus and mind their business. Is that right?"

Willow and Joseph nodded.

"Then I think y'all should leave them alone. That being said, Willow shot, probably killed, three of their men and I put a bullet through their leader. So peace might not be an option. All that being said, not my cow - not my farm."

Three Trustee Bots rounded the corner of a building to their south. They were galloping towards the crashed truck - weapons held high.

"You're right - not your farm." Willow said as she took off for the plaza.

Joseph and Gerti followed.

"If you're bent on destroying them, at least let me disable the chargers so we can come back later and salvage them." Joseph wasn't going to let her destroy something that was basically a magical source of electricity. Also, he might be able to keep her from doing another thing that couldn't be taken back later.

"Fine."

Another two Trustee Bots appeared to the south. They were searching - hunting.

The three of them moved north past the two buildings. They crouched down on the edge of the crumbling building and watched the courtyard for movement. There were four bots exchanging spots in the charging station that they had left operational.

Joseph started to make a move for the charging station when Gerti held him back. She pointed to the west.

There was a shirtless cadet running across the plaza. Joseph had a hard time making out the details but it looked like the cadet was covered in blood. He ran into a brick and concrete building on the far corner of the plaza.

"Okay, let's go." Willow made a run for the chargers - Gerti and Joseph followed. "How are you going to disable them?" Willow asked.

"I'm just going to disconnect the batteries from the solar cells. That should be all it takes. Help me climb up there." Joseph said, pointing to the panels on top of the station.

Gerti and Willow helped push him onto the roof.

The panels looked much worse during the day than they had the night before. He marveled at the engineering that must have gone into these to let them work after so many years.

Joseph reached underneath and felt around for the wiring harness that led down to the battery banks. He found it and pulled. The connectors resisted but finally parted.

There were three more he'd have to disconnect to sever the array completely. He was working on the fourth one when energy bolts whizzed through the plaza and made contact with the charging station. He turned to look. Four Trustee Bots were coming in from the south.

"Go that way!" Willow yelled to Gerti, pointing to the domed building.

Willow took off running west, her gun launching rounds at the bots as she ran.

149

Gerti took off running at a sprint.

Joseph put his belly to the top of the charging station and prayed that the little lip would be enough to hide him. He pulled the spare magazine out of his left pocket and reached for his pistol.

His holster was empty.

He cursed under his breath for forgetting it in the truck. He turned his head to watch the bots. Three of them followed Willow, their weapons flaring as they fired bolts of high-pitched screaming energy.

One of their chests erupted with sparks and it crumpled.

Willow had gotten into the building on the south western corner of the plaza. Her gun was still thundering. Joseph tried to press his body into the roof of the charging station further than reality would permit.

Two of Trustee Bots galloped into the plaza from the south. They moved towards the building where Willow was taking cover.

A thunderclap came from the domed building. Joe couldn't see it, but he heard a bot crumple to the east - probably the one that had been following Gerti.

Another heavy gunshot and the one closest to Willow was decommissioned.

Joseph imagined the ID tags in the control room blinking to red. The charging station started to shudder underneath him. The doors opened and four more

Trustee Bots stepped out. Joseph reached up and unplugged the last solar cell.

Thankfully, the connector separated without much fuss. He went to climb down the northern side of the charging station and was met with the shirtless cadet climbing up. Joseph stared at him - expecting him to pull a gun or something.

"Come on, we gotta get outta here." Clements said.

Joseph crawled along the roof without lifting his body up. He slipped over the edge with Clements guiding him.

"Thanks." Joseph said. "Hey, I'm sorry ab-"

"That wasn't your fault. We need to get inside." Clements must've been talking about the actual shooting instead of the inciting event. Joseph was willing to take the break if it was being offered.

They ran to a building on the northern edge but were met with three more bots. They turned to the east and ran to the domed building. Another bot appeared from behind a building. They were completely surrounded by bots intent on their deaths.

It started to say something - a muzzle flash from the second floor of the domed building - the bot's chest sprayed out the front of it.

They kept running until they were inside the building. They ran upstairs and found Gerti on the second floor. All the bots in the plaza were descending on Willow. Bursts of gunfire collided with them - turning them into jittering piles of scrap.

"I don't have enough ammo for this." Gerti muttered, chambering another round and firing.

The grenade bounced off the concrete ground and landed in the middle of three Trustee Bots. It erupted in a fiery explosion. Concrete and pieces of bot landed around the plaza and bounced off the roof of the charging station. Another short burst of gunfire came from one of the upper windows.

"I only saw three mags on her. I bet she's low too." Joseph said. .308 wasn't incredibly common and she had just blown through a lot of it. "I'm going to turn the bots off from the control room."

"No!" Brandon yelled.

"I have to. They're going to kill her." Joseph went to the stairwell and started climbing.

Clements followed him.

Joseph heard Gerti say something as he left the room but he couldn't hear what she said - his ears ringing from the gunfire.

Another throaty thunderclap rolled through the building. They reached the fourth floor. Clements ran ahead and blocked the hallway.

"Look. I can't let you do this! You heard the Commander - they would have killed me for what you did last night. I can't imagine what they'll do if you turn them off completely!" Clements yelled over the gunfire and ringing.

"I'm not gonna let them kill my friend."

"You can't - Please!"

Joseph paused. Tears were forming in Clement's eyes. His cheeks were flush and his chest had a sheen of sweat on it. Joseph tried to move past but Clements grabbed and pushed him into the wall of the hallway.

Joseph swung and made contact with Clements' ribs. He grimaced and punched Joseph in the head. Joseph had never really been in a fight - never really taken a hit before. His head spun as he stumbled backwards.

"You good? I don't want to fight I just -" Clements backed off a couple steps.

Joseph regained himself.

"Try to stop me again and I'll kill you." Joe said, holding his head.

Clements pressed his lips together and stood there. He was clearly thinking all of this through. Joseph realized that wasn't the best way to handle this situation but he didn't have enough time for careful diplomacy.

Joseph started to move sideways towards the supply closet with the ladder. Clements moved towards him - Joseph launched off the wall and tackled him. His left arm was wrapped around Clements and his right was striking anything it could. They careened through the broken glass door into the rotunda. The two of them rammed into the stone banister overlooking the seal and bell. Clements twisted away from it and they landed on the ground in a pile.

Clements screamed in pain and pulled his left arm in. Fresh blood oozed out of a freshly torn gash. He fought to crawl out from under Joseph.

The trooper bot stood in the hallway bearing its metallic fangs. Blood dripped from its maw.

"They're going to kill me." Clements said under his breath as he crawled away.

Joseph couldn't think of anything to say. He thought about telling him not to go back - or to come to Bryan - but he figured it would be useless. So he said nothing. Clements scrambled to his feet and backed up to the stairwell then disappeared down them.

"Thanks." Joseph said, looking down at the bot.

It relaxed its hunched stance and started wagging its tail stiffly. It squeaked in its socket.

Joseph carefully stepped over Liebowitz and climbed onto the roof. Once he was in the control room, he selected all the bots on the ID list and deactivated them.

* * *

Brandon worked his way through the campus until he made it back to the dorm. He had seen the bots deactivate and go limp - he knew he didn't have long before the other cadets noticed too. He realized this was probably a foolish hope. The cadets stationed on lookout duty would have noticed it immediately.

He ran as hard as his bruising body would let him.

The bots that surrounded the fallen cadets were sitting slumped over around the bodies. Their wooden rifles were still laying in the same spots.

"You look like shit." Hughes said when he saw Brandon run panting into the room.

He pulled the canister from his pocket and handed it to Grady. The doctor loaded the medgel into the applicator and started spraying into the exit wound.

They rolled the commander over and filled the entrance wound with the foam as well.

"Now we just wait." Dr. Grady said.

Helen Vaughn came running into the room.

"Dr. Grady!" With the Commander out of commission, Grady was the next in line of seniority. "The bots all turned off!"

"Send some of the cadets to the dining hall to look after the others. We'll need to be more alert until we can figure out what to do in the long run. Can you get the message out?" he asked.

"Yessir." She nodded and left the room.

"Hughes, Jacob, give us the room."

They nodded and went into the hallway.

He closed the door behind them. It was just Grady, Brandon, and Commander Rose in the room now. The latter wasn't in a conscious state.

"Rose will want to see you dead." Grady said.

"I know."

"You need to get out of here before he comes to."

"I know."

"Hughes was right. You do look like shit."

"I know."

Grady sprayed a little of the medgel onto Brandon's torn arm and wrapped it in a bandage.

"Take your rifle and anything you can carry," he ordered.

"They took my rifle when I came on as your assistant."

"Ah, that's right." He thought for a moment. "I have a pistol in my side table upstairs - and a box of ammo. Take them - I don't need 'em."

"Thank you."

"You've been a good student."

"You've been a good teacher." Brandon's heart hurt more than his body. He'd have to leave his home, his family, the protection of the campus...

"Go somewhere you can use what you've learned." Dr. Grady said.

Brandon nodded and left the makeshift clinic.

He slipped upstairs into Dr. Grady's room and retrieved an old revolver from his bedside table. He opened the cylinder and loaded six rounds from the box labeled .38 Special. He dropped the box and the revolver into his pockets and went to his room. He put on a white undershirt, grabbed a handful of clothes and his medical kit. He stuffed all this into a backpack and threw it over his shoulder.

He thought about going to the dining hall and saying goodbye to his little sister and dad but he didn't want them to know he was leaving. He stepped back into the room with Dr. Grady.

"Will you tell my family I left and that I'll be okay?" he asked.

"Of course."

Brandon took a deep breath and nodded thanks before heading out the door and entering the greater world.

Chapter Ten
September 25th, 2114
Bryan, Texas
Girl

Joe, Willow and Gerti had gotten back later the day they left.

They even brought back a cute little robot dog that seemed to like her. It followed Joe around during the day while he was working. The Mayor, Frank, had given her a small stack of green coins to use for the week while she recovered.

She was sitting in the cafe while Mrs. Laredo rushed around behind the counter getting ready for dinner. Harrison, the doctor, had told the girl to stay off her leg as much as possible until tomorrow.

She felt bad about watching while Mrs. Laredo worked by herself but that was better than sitting alone in Joe's, or Gloria's, apartment waiting for the day to end.

Willow had talked Gerti into sticking around for a few days to help out with guard duty. Apparently her husband, Miguel, and a few of the other guards were sent to the shelter to trade crystals for supplies. The girl was relieved Gerti had stayed on while she recovered.

"Do you want your supper now or do you want to wait for the others?" she asked.

"I'll wait, thank you though." The girl was the only other person in the cafe.

Mrs. Laredo sighed, looked around at the empty kitchen, then walked over and sat down besides the girl.

"Just gonna take a little break before everyone comes in," she said with a smile. "How long are you stayin'? In town, I mean."

"I was thinking about leaving with Gerti - whenever she goes back to Waco."

"I just hate the idea of you two girls out there by yourselves."

"Thanks Mrs. Laredo, but I've been on the road as long as I can remember and Gerti seems pretty capable."

"Y'all both seem capable but I'll still be prayin' for y'all when you leave. I was just thinking - Jacob could use another guard like your friend. And we could use some more entertainment than just Lucas. Not to mention, I could use more help 'round here. Bryan needs people like the two of you."

"Are you offering me a job?" the girl asked, grinning.

"Well Sweetheart, I was thinking of it as me offerin' a home - to both of you."

Someone tried to turn the handle to the shop but it rattled. She quickly went and unlocked it. People started filtering in.

The first group that walked in was the religious leader, Pastor Gene, and his family. There was his wife, Mary, and their three kids. Martha, George, and their youngest, Alex. Alex seemed like a good kid. He had come into the cafe yesterday and taught the girl how to play a game called Speed with a set of playing cards he had made with thick paper his Dad had bought from the shelter.

There was Dr. Harrison Gardner and his wife Alysia. They were a good looking couple. Harrison had been gentle when he was examining her leg. Alysia was sweet and brought her sweeter tea during the exam.

An older man with long gray hair and a large leather coat slung over his arm came in, got his meal, and sat down in the corner by himself. He looked grumpy - or tired.

Alex said something to his dad then all three of Pastor's kids ran over and sat down with the old man. He greeted them and they began talking animatedly.

"Pastor, will you say grace?" Mrs. Laredo asked.

He nodded then everyone in the room closed their eyes and looked down. He began talking to someone. He thanked them for the food and for the safety they were able to enjoy. The girl had learned a long time ago not to question people's practices - especially if it wasn't hurting anyone. He said amen and the small crowd returned to their meals.

The rusty trooper model came running in. Joe, Gloria, and Lucas came in after it. Joe still had a nasty blackeye from where Clements had gotten one in on him.

The Trooper ran up and put its muzzle on the girl's knee. She laughed and rubbed its head. She got up and they joined the others in line.

"How was work?" the girl asked.

"Shit." Lucas said.

"Yeah, it's been annoying. We're trying to pull the Treighl converters out and connect them to our grid - but they're all so damaged it's hard to get 'em out without tearin' 'em up." Joe said.

They got their food and sat down. It was finely shredded chicken, pickles, and some fruit in a cold creamy sauce.

"Ah, mana." Joe said as he started eating.

"Hey, who's the guy talking to Pastor's kids?" the girl asked.

"That's Anshin, he used to be a Diurnal hunter." Joe said. "He'd break into shelters that were abandoned after the fires."

Mrs. Laredo walked up with two jars filled with whatever they had just eaten.

"Will one of y'all take this to Gerti and Willow in the north tower?" she asked.

"Of course." Joe said, taking the jars of food.

"We can take it." the girl said, motioning to Gloria and herself.

Gloria had been kind enough to house the girl while they were staying. Her apartment was only a short walk away from the north gate and guard tower. Gerti was staying with Willow. Gloria nodded, agreeing to the task.

They finished their food and got up.

"Tomorrow - I'm getting off work a little early. Do you want to practice?" Lucas asked the girl. The town got together on Wednesday nights and Lucas would play the guitar. The girl had agreed to sing with him next time they all got together.

More townspeople filtered in to get their allotment of dinner.

* * *

"You ever regret doing something you were told?" Willow asked.

Gerti turned and looked at her. They had been sitting in peaceful silence for the last three hours.

"I felt bad the first time I killed someone." Gerti offered.

"Why'd you do it?"

"I was out hunting - it had to've only been my second time out by myself - two men tried to attack me. I shot one of them and the other ran away."

"Why'd you feel bad about that?"

"I was a kid. I don't know. I think killing someone is supposed to be difficult though."

"Maybe. Didn't seem like you had a problem the other day."

Gerti shrugged.

"That's not what I was thinking of anyway. I meant, have you ever done something - I don't know how to say this. When someone tells you - someone you're supposed to listen to - tells you do something wrong - and you do it - it doesn't really feel like it's your fault because they told you to do it. But you still did it and you have to live with that feeling." Willow rolled her index finger in a slow circle as she was talking - trying to work through what she meant.

Gerti took a slow breath and considered how to proceed.

"Why?" she finally asked. This felt like it was going to be a floodgate kinda conversation. The kind you just listen to and let the other person figure it out while they talk. Maybe.

"Just something I've been thinking about recently. I know that's gotta sound bad."

"You're trying to find your line?" Gerti asked.

"Exactly." Willow said under her breath.

"Well, what's your line?"

"I don't know."

"It's important to know before you get there."

"What do you mean?"

"I mean, if you think *someone* is going to ask you to do something that crosses your line, you need to decide now whether or not you will. It's hard to tell if they've already asked and you're struggling with it or if you're just expecting it but -" Willow opened her mouth - Gerti held her hand up to cut her off. "You don't have to tell me. You're obviously under a lot of pressure. But it's that pressure that will guide your decision in the moment. That's why it's so important to decide beforehand."

Having witnessed Willow effortlessly cut down three men, Gerti shuddered to imagine what order would cross her moral line. But who was she to judge - she had killed her fair share. She had even shot to kill during that fight too.

Willow shifted the rifle in her lap.

"Do you know your line?" Willow asked.

"The council has a… job board - well a task list that bears can choose from if they don't want to do the job assigned to them. They're all very dangerous of course. The job they assigned me was to kill a guy named Bezral Gropht. He's one of the elders in the outer community and he doesn't get along with the council - anyway, I couldn't do that and I was afraid that they'd assign me somethin' like that. Just to prove my loyalty. So, I said I wouldn't do it. They were fine with that of course - they were just filtering people out. But that left me with two options - I could choose one of their dangerous tasks or they could execute me on the spot."

"So you came to university."

"Yeah, well, I didn't realize it was just an extended death sentence."

"Did you warn Gropht?"

"No. I would've but he probably already knows he's on their list. Anyway, if I had they'd have killed me and my family - or at least added us to the list with him."

"Had you made that decision before they asked you?" Willow asked.

"Yeah. Like I said the other day, I had worked for them for a while but it was all small stuff - guarding places, patrolling the streets, you know? I figured they would try to test me with something - I just didn't know what."

"What's gonna happen when you walk in there with whatever you found?"

"I - I don't know." She hadn't considered that.

Footsteps approached the guard tower. They turned around to see who it was.

"Y'all want supper?" Gloria asked. She handed up the two containers.

Gwen struggled to climb up into the small tower's ladder. She leaned up against one of the posts while the two of them ate. Gloria climbed up the ladder and rested her arms on the floor.

"How much longer do y'all have?" Gloria asked.

"Couple hours. Jordan's got next." Willow said through a yawn. "Sorry, I don't sleep well when Miguel's gone."

"I'll be alright if you want to take off." Gerti said.

"Nah, Jacob wants two sets of eyes up here during the day - because of all the cadet stuff."

"I can stay." Gwen said.

Willow thought a moment before nodding and standing up. She took the magazine out of her gun, emptied the chamber, loaded the round into the magazine, and handed it to Gwen.

"Fire select's here. Keep it single shot, I only have two magazines left. And thanks. Gerti, I'll leave the door unlocked for you."

Gloria got out of the way as Willow climbed down. Gwen picked up the rifle and looked it over before sitting. She peeked over her shoulder to make sure Willow was gone.

"What were y'all talking about before we came up?" Gwen asked.

"Why?"

"Her eyes were all puffy." Gloria said.

"Oh." Gerti hadn't noticed but she and Willow hadn't been looking at each other. "We were talking about where we draw our moral lines - and she's worried about Miguel. Sounded like she had a lot on her mind."

The three of them sat in silence for a few minutes.

The road in front of them had been cleared. All the cars had been pushed to the sides and torn down for metal. There was an open field to the right and a large neighborhood of cracked and bare foundations to the left. Not too many places to hide.

There was a dull roar of thunder far to the south of them.

"I've heard them arguing about that - the moral line stuff. I think so anyway." Gloria said.

Gerti kept her eye on the horizon but she heard Gwen shift in her chair to look at Gloria.

"I was walking back from Harold's last week and I heard them arguing in the guard tower. Miguel didn't want her to do whatever it was but she said she had to. I didn't want them to know I was listening so I got outta there." Gloria said.

"Will you ask her about it?" Gwen asked.

"Me?" Gerti asked.

Gwen nodded.

"I'll ask if it comes up." Gerti said, leaning back into her chair.

"It sounds like she needs help. I can ask if you're uncomfortable doing it." Gwen said.

"No, I wouldn't want her to know we've been talkin' 'bout it."

"Mkay, well, we have an early morning tomorrow. So I'm gonna go home - if y'all are alright?" Gloria asked.

"Yeah, we'll be alright." Gwen said.

Gloria climbed down and walked a little ways south to her apartment.

"Hey, Mrs. Laredo asked if we would stay here. She offered me a job at the cafe and said they wanted you to stay on working for the town."

"I have to get back home." Gerti said, thinking about the little plastic thing in her pocket.

"I know. I just wanted to let you know." Gwen said.

"Thanks. Are you still wantin' to come with me?

"Yeah, I like this place but it just doesn't feel right."

"What do you mean?"

"I don't know - just a feeling. And all that stuff about Willow doesn't help."

"Alright, we'll get outta here as soon as you're good."

"Thanks for waiting." Gwen said, smiling.

They sat in silence until a young black man came to relieve them and start his night shift. He yawned and pulled out a cigarette as he settled into place. The two girls said goodnight to Jordan and went their separate ways for the night.

Chapter Eleven
September 26th, 2114
Bryan, Texas
Joseph Marion

Joseph woke up to a knock on his door. He threw his covers off and ignored Purcevile's complaints. It was dark out. The trooper bot perked its ears and sniffed at the door. Joseph's watch showed it was a little after midnight. He looked through the peephole and saw Gloria standing there with a lit electric lantern. She looked tired - tired and pissed. She knocked again. Joseph opened the door.

"You left your radio off. Allen's calling us to the cafe. Something's wrong with the power." She turned before Joseph could answer and walked down the stairs.

Joseph got dressed, grabbed his tool bag, and left his apartment - the trooper following in his footsteps. The moon was a thin sliver and dark clouds raced across the sky. The wind blew hard through the streets and the air smelled like rain. Lights were on in the cafe when he approached it. Allen and Lucas were already looking through the breaker panels in the little closet.

"Gloria, will you go up and check out the batteries? Joe, go with her - see what y'all can find." Allen said.

They left the cafe and climbed the stairs to the top floor of the parking garage. They had decided it made more sense to put the battery banks on the top floor, instead of the roof, and leave the new solar arrays where the old ones were. It required a little more cable but that's something they had - and they figured the security outweighed the cost.

"What the hell?" Gloria asked, holding her lantern over the batteries.

Joseph put his flashlight on them. Something had smashed two batteries. Whatever did it had unplugged them from the battery array harness first. The air smelled like a thunderstorm and Joseph could feel the hair on his arm standing straight up.

"We have a few spare, right?" Gloria asked.

"Yeah, if they're still there." Joseph went to the stairwell and found two spares on the top landing. He brought them back and reconnected them.

Gloria's radio squawked.

"Hey, whatever y'all did fixed it." Allen said over the radio.

Joseph unclipped his radio and held it up.

171

"Hey Allen, y'all should come up here." Joseph carefully pulled the damaged batteries out of their spots and lowered a new one into place. The old batteries were leaking a light blue fluid and the inside was filled with metal plates. He'd never seen battery acid that looked like that but he didn't know what Treighl got up to with their tech.

His flashlight reflected off the metal plates. There were small sections that didn't reflect as much - in fact, those sections looked like they were absorbing the light. He reached out to move one of the plates - to get a closer look at these strange spots.

"Hey, careful." Gloria said.

Joseph nodded but moved his hand closer anyway.

A blue bolt of electricity shot from the plate into his hand. He yelped out of surprise and pulled his hand back. His hand and arm were tingling but it felt different than when he'd been shocked in the past.

Direct current always felt dull - alternating current always felt sharp and painful. This was a penetrating feeling that went through his entire body - like what he thought jumping into a cup of ice water would feel like.

He could almost feel it reverberate off his left foot and start to come back up before it dissipated re-entering his chest. His heart was racing and he could feel the adrenaline making him vibrate.

"You good?" Gloria asked.

"I feel great." He reached out to touch it again. It shocked him again but nowhere near as much. He turned over the plate and examined the weird patches. They were symbols etched into the metal - some of them were the same symbols he had seen inside the solar cells.

The blue fluid moved.

Slowly, like living slime, it started to pull towards his hand. A section of the fluid accumulated and began to lift upwards towards his fingers. He dropped the plate and leaned away from the battery. He didn't know what the hell that was but he didn't want it touching him - he had seen enough movies to know this was bad. Allen and Lucas came through the stairwell door.

"What's up?" Allen asked.

"Someone smashed the batteries." Gloria said.

Allen walked over and looked at the destroyed batteries.

"Don't touch them. They shocked the hell outta me." Joseph said, pointing to the viscous blue gel that had fallen back into a normal puddle inside the cracked plastic case.

"Why would someone…" Allen started, looking angrily at the batteries. He pulled out his radio and changed the channel. "Hey Jordan, you got ears on?" Allen asked into his radio.

A couple seconds later Jordan said he did.

"Someone smashed a couple of the new batteries." Allen said. "Get some of the other guards to check around town - make sure everyone's okay. We're going to make sure there's nobody in the parking tower then join y'all."

"Sure thing, Al."

"Okay, split up and make sure the garage is clear. Keep your ears on and call if you see anyone. Once we're done here, go to the cafe and we'll go from there. Y'all armed?" He reached into his pocket and pulled out his glock.

Everyone pulled out their weapons. Lucas had his dad's old .44 revolver and Gloria had her .38. The trooper made a low growl. Joseph smiled.

"Good. Ears on - eyes open. I'm going to check out the roof then come back down." He went into the stairwell and disappeared up the stairs.

Lucas started heading for the other stairwells.

Gloria and Joseph worked their way down the parking garage one floor at a time - their pistols aimed at every darting shadow.

Most of the cars had been cleared out for scrap metal but there were still a few burnt out husks left where they were last parked. Joseph could hear the others moving through the parking garage - at least he hoped that's who he heard.

Something moved behind a car to his right. He swung his pistol and light towards it. Whatever it was disappeared - it was probably just his imagination.

The trooper kept moving down the sloped floor before it realized Joseph had stopped. Joseph orbited the car and looked underneath the burnt up hull. Satisfied that he was hunting shadows - he moved on.

Gloria and Joseph made it to the bottom around the same time. Lucas and Allen weren't out yet. They walked together to the cafe. His watch claimed it had only been forty minutes since Gloria had woken him up. It felt like it had been much longer.

"Who do you think it was?" Gloria asked.

"I don't know." Joseph couldn't think of anyone who had anything to gain from partially disabling the power. The cadets might try to disable it completely - as part of revenge or an attack. But why partially?

"Lucas probably did it so he could kill Harold." Gloria muttered.

"Harold's still has power." Joseph laughed - as if that was the only defense for Lucas.

"What if it was that cadet guy?" She offered. Joseph shrugged. A flashlight flickered over them. They turned to see Jacob walking up - he lowered his rifle and light when he saw who they were.

"Allen down yet?" he asked.

"No sir. He and Lucas are still in the parking garage. They haven't radioed anything though." Joseph said.

"Alright. Joe, go ahead and grab your long arm - just in case things get difficult. I'll go check on Allen and Lucas." Jacob started jogging towards the garage.

Joseph pulled up his radio.

"Allen and Lucas, Jacob is heading to the parking garage."

"Mkay - thanks." Allen called on the radio.

Joseph and Gloria went to his apartment and grabbed his shotgun.

"Let's go get Gwen." Gloria said.

"Could use the extra eyes. I'm sure Willow and Gerti are on their way already."

Gloria's apartment was a little shop in a row of wall to wall one story buildings. Pieces of sheet metal were riveted over where there had once been windows. Missing bricks had been replaced with little piles of river rocks held in place with dried mud. Her door had been repaired with old scorched fence boards.

It was wide open - the power was out inside.

"Gwen?" Gloria called out into the darkness. There wasn't an answer.

Joseph handed the pump shotgun to Gloria and pulled out his pistol and flashlight. He entered the little apartment.

The sheets on Gloria's bed were still thrown to the side. There were some blankets and a pillow on the couch. The blankets were disturbed and Gwen was nowhere to be seen. They moved through the dark apartment but there weren't too many places Gwen could've hidden.

"Gwen?" Joseph called.

"Maybe Gerti already got her. I bet they're helping check on people."

"Maybe." Joseph said, lowering his pistol.

They left the apartment and went back to the cafe. Allen, Lucas, Jacob, Willow, and Gerti were already there. Allen, Lucas, and Jacob were discussing what to do while Gerti and Willow scanned the area.

"Have you seen Gwen?" Gloria asked Gerti.

"No, is she not at your place?"

"We went to get her - nowhere to be seen." Joseph said.

"Lucas said someone smashed the batteries? Maybe it was her?" Willow said.

"Why would she do that?" Gloria asked.

"I don't know - just seems odd, that happens and then she's gone." Willow said.

"If she was going to leave, why would she need to have a distraction?" Joseph asked.

"She was planning on going with me back to Waco. I don't think she would leave in the middle of the night like this."

"Maybe y'all didn't know her as well as you thought." The mayor walked up to the group. He had a hunting rifle slung over his shoulder. He had mud on his shoes and he was sweating. He must've run here from his house at the south gate.

"Sir, we're planning on going door to door to make sure everyone's in their homes." Jacob said.

"Let's get to it. Where do you need me?" he asked.

"You don't have to help us. We have it under control." Allen said.

"Nonsense," he said, unlimbering his rifle.

They split up into groups of two and went to everyone's homes. It was well into five in the morning before they were finished.

Everyone, except Gwen, was accounted for. Gloria said she wasn't comfortable sleeping in her apartment and asked Joseph if she could sleep at his place. She slept on the couch and he slept on the floor in the corner - he always preferred to have his back against a wall. The trooper curled up at the end of the couch and kept its eyes on the door of Joseph's apartment.

* * *

Gerti stood in the middle of Gloria's apartment and took it all in. There was something here and she wanted to figure it out.

The sheets on the couch had been dragged off and were lying on the floor. Gerti walked around the room until she came to the front door. She ran her fingers along the burnt wooden frame - it was still intact next to where the deadbolt went in. The doorknob latched and the lock still worked. She closed the door and looked at the door frame from the inside.

There was a pretty sizable gap between the door and the frame. She rolled the lock back and forth a couple times. She watched the bolt enter and exit the metal stop plate.

Gerti checked the window in the bathroom - it was nailed shut. She pulled on every piece of metal and every board that covered the front shop windows - nothing budged - Gloria had locked this place tight. She examined the door again looking for any sign of forced entry or any clue that would suggest someone else was here last night. She pursed her lips and frowned.

People were hard to predict - maybe Gwen had just left. Maybe she got freaked out by how nice everyone was being to her. Gerti tensed her jaw and shook her head. Who knows. She was looking forward to the company on the way home but she would be fine. Why would Gwen have talked to her about going to Waco then just leave? It didn't make any sense. Metallic clattering outside preceded the trooper bot trotting up - Joe followed it in.

"Find anything?" he asked.

She shook her head.

"You?"

"Everyone was where they were supposed to be and nobody saw anything last night. Jordan was on north watch - you know - he didn't see anything here. I bet she just took off." he said, shaking his head in return.

"Just doesn't feel right."

"Frank's probably right. None of us 've really spent that much time together."

"Yeah, I guess. What about the batteries though? Why would she've done that?"

"Gloria says she was still here whenever Allen called on the radio. Well, she says she thinks Gwen was here - it was dark."

"How long were the coolers off before Allen made the call?"

"I really couldn't tell ya," he said with a shrug.

Gerti closed her eyes, put her hands in her pockets, and took a deep breath. How long was she willing to spend on this? She felt the plastic meal tokens clicking off each other in her pocket. She pulled her left arm out and looked at her wrist before looking at Joe with a questioning expression.

He smirked and checked his watch.

"Nine seventeen."

"Let's get something to eat. I need to think about all this."

They walked down the road, past Joe's apartment, towards the cafe.

The trooper ran past the cafe and around the corner of the row of old businesses. It popped its head back around the corner and looked at them. It made a mechanical whirring and whining noise.

Joe started to call the bot back to them but Gerti held her hand up. She pointed at the bot and tilted her head. It was acting like it knew something.

Joe's eyes widened and he nodded. The bot did a little hop when they walked towards it. Gerti grinned at the little canine affectations the robot had been programmed to do.

They followed the trooper towards the city hall and the parking garage.

After crossing the old railroad tracks, the bot peeled off towards the south and started following the fence when it got there. The bot stopped at the spot they came in through the wall. It circled and jumped at the board that needed to be moved. Gerti was impressed that it remembered the spot and then she felt a little silly. It wasn't actually a dog of course. She wondered what other things were permanently burned into the bot's hard drives.

Joe pulled the boards back and it jumped through - they followed.

"Hey, we could've gone through the main gates - it's the day." Joe said.

181

The bot stopped, turned around, and made eye contact with Joe before turning back around and continuing.

"'Kay." Joe chuckled.

They followed it a few blocks to a brick and concrete building. They had passed it on the way in - the shop where they had left the Treighl bots in was just across the street to the east.

The bot was trotting along when it suddenly stopped. It paced around in a ten-by-ten area before making a whining noise and sitting down. It looked up at Gerti and Joe. Its eyebrows were articulating to make a worried expression.

"Were you following something?" Gerti asked.

The bot let out a small yip.

"Did you lose it?" She asked. The bot yipped again.

"Does that mean yes?" Joe asked. The bot yipped again.

"Oh. Well, I guess that's not actually very conclusive," he said, rubbing his forehead.

"Let's go in there and look around. It had to've come here for a reason." Gerti pointed to the building.

There was a circle driveway in the corner of the L shaped building. They crossed a short stone wall and approached its front doors. All the windows had been boarded up or filled in with stone and concrete. There were two sets of mud tracks leading to the front of the building - straight to the doors.

"What do y'all use this for?" Gerti asked.

"We don't use it for anything. Not that I know of anyway."

"Well, someone's fixed it up and been here recently," she said, pointing at the windows and the footprints.

The glass front doors were in the back of a recessed entry walkway. They had been covered over with pieces of rebar that had been welded onto the metal frame. The air inside the walkway smelled funny - almost like baked corn - and there was a musky smell alongside it. She knew the smell but couldn't think where she knew it from.

Gerti looked in through the bars. There was a small entry area that opened up into the rest of the building. Something moved inside. She caught a glimpse of orange fur in the darkness. She jumped back from the door. There had been a time when she was hunting with her Mom and they came across a, thankfully empty, tiger den.

"Joe, why the hell are there tigers?" she asked.

"Tigers?"

A low growl came from inside the building. They both looked through the bars to see a tiger peer around the corner of the entryway walls. Its head was thick and its mouth was open as it growled. The muddy footprints went by where the tiger was standing. The creature stopped growling before it let out a loud guttural hissing.

"Whoa. You got it, Chief." Joe said, as he backed away from the door.

The tiger slowly approached the door and pressed its teeth against the bars as it growled at them.

Gerti stayed where she was - she figured the bars were close enough together that the tiger wouldn't be able to get one of its meaty arms through. She looked at the coloration of the tiger's eyes. They were a yellowish orange which meant the tiger was normal and not mutated.

She had heard about mutated tigers having acid spit and metal claws - among other horrendous things. The tiger's maw was a mere foot from her face.

She looked down to study the foot prints. One was a smooth soled boot and the other looked like a hiking boot or combat boot. They were both decent sized but not clearly a man's or a woman's - based on the size at least. She figured there was a way to tell but she wasn't used to reading human tracks.

"You sure you don't know anything about this?" Gerti asked.

"Yeah. I promise. What do you think's in there?"

"I don't know but did your parents ever use the phrase *'weird-shit-o-meter?'*"

"No, but I follow."

Chapter Twelve
2114
Girl

The girl was sitting alone on a wooden stage in a darkened theater - the front row of red velvet seats barely visible through the harsh beams of the stage lights. She was sitting in a wooden chair with her arms tied down at her sides. Someone was sitting in the front row. Navy slacks and brown dress shoes - one casually crossed over the other.

She raised a hand to block the lights but the lone audience member was still obfuscated by the hazy darkness. There was a sharp pinch at the crook of her right arm. She looked down and was surprised to see that her scars were missing.

"Don't worry about that," a man's voice came from the darkness.

She tried to speak - tried to ask where she was and who they were. She opened her mouth but nothing came out.

"Think of somewhere - anywhere you want." She tried to think of a place she wanted to go but couldn't. She could remember visiting the Gulf Basin shore - it was pretty but not somewhere she would necessarily want to see again.

There was the castle at the Fairegrounds.

The flats that lead down into the Atlantic.

The classroom at the university.

The cafe.

Gloria's apartment.

The girl stood up from the couch in Gloria's living room. Gerti and Gloria were sitting at the coffee table holding cards. Joe was leaning against the counter in the kitchen laughing at something. The three of them were frozen. What was Joe laughing at?

The girl remembered Gloria saying something funny. Something about 'definitely not' having a pair of aces in her hand. They had stopped playing before they showed their hands.

There had been an ace on the table and the girl was pretty sure Gloria had just been joking - especially since the girl actually did have two aces in her hand.

She walked around the table and looked at Gloria's hand of cards - not a single ace. The girl grinned and checked the cards in the middle of the table. All the numbers were missing and the queen of spades, that had been there that night, was replaced with an ID card with the picture of an elderly hispanic woman.

The girl looked at the cards in Gloria's hand again - five aces were fanned out evenly. The fifth had a square instead of the normal suits and was colored blue. She blinked and the cards were a completely different set.

"Do you enjoy poker?" the voice asked.

"I had never played it before," she answered, relieved to have her voice back. She had her voice back but it didn't feel like she was the one pushing the words out. The room slowly faded away as they talked.

"What games do you play?" it asked.

"I used to play a lot of chess."

"What made you stop?"

"I ran."

"Ran? From what?"

"I don't know."

"Think."

"Home."

"Sure. Tell me about your parents."

"No."

"Tell me about your parents."

"No."

"Tell me about your siblings."

"I don't think I have any."

"Why do you think that?"

"My Mom died right after I was born."

"Maybe you had older siblings?"

"They died when they were born."

"Who told you that?"

"My Dad."

"Were the two of you close?"

"When I was little."

"What changed?"

"He died."

"I'm sorry. What happened to him?"

"I killed him."

"I'm sure you had your reasons."

"I did."

"What were they?"

"He hurt me."

"How?"

"Cut me up. So I cut him up."

"How old were you?"

"I was a kid."

"Why did he hurt you?"

"He said it was because I cheated."

"How did you cheat?"

"I would look at what he was going to do."

"Before he did it?"

"Yes."

"Can you still do that? Can you still see what people are going to do before they do it?"

"No."

"Well that's a shame, Gwen."

"My name's not Gwen."

"Oh? What is it?"

"I don't know."

"What'd your dad call you?"

"Demon. Monster. Abomination. God's mistake."

"What did your mom call you?"

"She didn't name me - she thought I was going to die like the others."

"What was the first thing your Dad called you?"

"He called me Kid, Child, or Girl. He told me that I could die at any moment and what's the point of naming something that's just going to die."

"He thought of you like that but still played chess with you? You would still say y'all were close before you killed him?"

"He went back and forth. He'd be really nice for a while then he'd be really cruel for a while. When I got older he stopped being nice."

"I'm sorry you had to deal with that."

"It's alright. Hey, who are you?"

"Don't worry about that. I'm taking care of you.

"Oh. Okay. Where am I?"

"You're safe."

"But where am I?"

The voice didn't answer and the girl realized there was nothing around her. She was floating in total darkness - what she imagined space to be like.

She blinked and she was surrounded by an infinite field of distant stars. She turned her head and saw Earth below her. She had never seen the Earth like this before - obviously. She had never been to space - nobody had. She had seen old maps of the planet but this was very different. The land was much larger and the blue of the water was farther out. Dark swirling clouds covered the Gulf of Mexico.

The sand shifted beneath her feet as she looked out into the muddy brown water. She looked back and saw the metal city lying partially submerged in the sand. An old structure from before the fires that used to float on the surface of the water. She laid down in the sand and rested her head in her hands. She took a deep breath and tried to calm down. If she was dreaming she really needed to wake up.

The sand beneath her became soft fabric. She opened her eyes and saw she was now in a small room with a bed for two. There was a window to her right with a floral curtain closing out the light. Yellowed wallpaper had been burned and peeled off various spots on the wall.

She felt movement on the bed next to her. She looked and saw Willow sitting hunched over on the side of the bed with her head in her hands.

There was an aura of sadness around her that the girl could physically feel. The crying was a dead giveaway too but the aura sealed it. She watched Willow crying for quite a while before she finally got up, threw her rifle over her shoulder, and left.

The ghostly sound of crying persisted even after Willow had left.

The girl turned around to see a little girl crying in a dark corner of the room. Except the room wasn't the hotel anymore. It was her old room where her dad had kept her after he found out about the mind cheating.

She sat down next to her younger self. There was a small wooden chess board folded up and stuffed under the young girl's legs.

"Hey, you're gonna be okay, Kid," she said, while gently pulling the chess board out. She flipped it open and started removing the plastic pieces. "Wanna play a game?" she asked.

The young girl sucked in her tears and nodded.

"Alright, let's get out of here," the older girl said.

The room shifted into the cafe in Bryan. It was empty. They sat down at a table and began playing. Several turns into the game, the young girl saw something behind the older girl and jumped.

"What are you doing? Teaching my little girl to cheat?" her dad yelled.

He was a gruff looking man with shaggy brown hair and a faded green winter jacket. He grabbed the edges of the table to flip it but froze before he could.

"This is your world. You can do whatever you want while you're here." It was the voice from earlier.

The girl pictured what she wanted and it appeared. The chess board was gone and had been replaced by a deck of playing cards. Her dad was sitting in the vacant third chair smiling at his daughters.

"Alright, some friends of mine taught me how to play poker. I can show both of you if you want?" she asked.

"Of course, Sweetheart," her dad said happily.

* * *

Gerti, Joe, and the trooper were walking back through the gap in the wall. They had circled the building that Joe said was the old police station, according to the sign, looking for another way in. All the windows were filled with stone and concrete - all the doors had been removed and blocked with stone as well. Unless there was a door on the roof, the only easy way in was through the front. Gerti caught Joe's eye and motioned to her wrist.

"Little after four," he answered.

Gerti wanted to spend some time thinking about this. Maybe get some help.

There was a ruckus coming from the street in front of Harold's. They jogged down the alley to see what was going on.

"You heard what I said!" Harold yelled.

Lucas and Jacob were holding each of the man's arms as he struggled against them. Lucas kicked the back of Harold's left knee - he hit the ground.

"Lucas!" Jacob yelled, while helping Harold to his feet.

"You're gonna -" Harold started.

"Harold, just shut your mouth, man." Jacob said tiredly.

A small crowd of people had come out of their buildings to see what was going on. Willow and Jordan stood nearby - they were both armed but their rifles were still slung over their shoulders.

"Everybody go back inside - everything's fine." Jacob called out.

Nobody moved.

Jacob sighed and started moving Harold towards the old office next to the cafe. They had a few sturdy rooms in there that they used as jail cells when the need arose.

Lucas started to follow but Willow stepped forward and held a hand out to stop him. He opened his mouth to say something but decided not to.

Willow pursed her lips and shook her head. Gerti thought she looked disappointed in the guy. Willow and Jordan followed after Jacob and Harold.

"Hey man, what's going on?" Joe asked, walking up to Lucas.

"That jackass snuck into my house when the power was out - while we were goin' house to house - stole a bunch of stuff. They think he's the one that jacked with the batteries."

194

"Who thinks that?" Joe asked.

"Frank and Jacob - Allen too."

"So they think he messed with the batteries to get you out of the house?" Gerti asked.

Lucas nodded.

"Why wouldn't he've just gone while you were at practice?" Gerti asked.

"Huh?" Lucas said.

"You and Gwen were going to practice music tonight, right?"

"Oh… Yeah?" Lucas said, clearly having forgotten.

"Then why would he need to cause all the damage?"

"I don't know - maybe he didn't know about that. All I know is, the power went out and then a bunch of mine and Krystal's stuff ends up at his place. My door was also broken through last night while we were out. It's not hard to put two and two together."

"How'd you find out he had your things?" Gerti asked.

"I - I came over to talk with Krystal." Lucas pointed to the barbershop.

Krystal was standing behind the heavy wooden door barely visible through a pane of glass.

Gerti narrowed her eyes. She thought about prodding more but decided she didn't want to get into a fist fight.

"Sounds like you just wanted to start somethin'." Joe said quietly.

Lucas immediately swung at Joe - he raised his hands to block but didn't quite make it.

Knuckles cracked as they smashed into Joe's jaw.

She quickly stepped between the two of them before anything else could happen. The trooper bot lunged at Lucas - he jumped back and pulled his revolver. The bot growled but stayed where it was.

"What the hell?" Allen yelled, as he ran up.

Gloria was following a distance back.

"He was running his mouth." Lucas said.

"Were you?" Allen asked.

Joe shrug-nodded.

"Hm." Allen turned back to Lucas. "Go home."

"I need to talk with Krystal first," he said, walking towards the barbershop.

Allen grabbed his wrist and pulled him off balance.

He stopped and turned to Allen.

"You're gonna go home - now." Allen said, looking the man in the eyes.

They stared at each other for a few moments.

Lucas let out a deep breath, holstered his revolver, and walked off towards the hotel. Allen watched him walking until he rounded the corner of the tall building. He turned to Joe.

"You good?" he asked.

Joe shrug-nodded again.

Allen shook his head and walked off - still shaking his head. Gerti looked at Joe's face. A fresh bruise was forming under the ones Clements had given him.

"What happened?" Gloria asked.

"'s bein' an ass. 's usual." Joe said. He put a hand to his temple and rubbed it gently.

"Mmm. Let's get you off your feet, Bud." Gerti said.

She and Gloria helped him back to his apartment and laid him down on the couch. Gerti pulled the shades over the large window. The trooper approached Gerti and shook its body back and forth.

"You good?" She asked.

The bot swung its flank out hard enough that it popped a service panel out. It was being held in place by four rusted stripped screws that hadn't been put back in all the way.

"You need some work done?" she asked, chuckling.

The bot yipped.

Gerti waved Gloria over to look at it. She chuckled when she saw the loose screws.

"Classic," she said, grabbing a screwdriver from Joe's desk. She took the screws out and removed the panel. There was a small screen and a few tiny buttons set into a metal plate. Gloria pressed one and began navigating the options on the screen.

"What's it say?" Gerti asked.

"There's an error - something about memory files. Well, something about displaying memory files." Gloria said.

She prodded around for a second then raised an eyebrow. She grabbed the screwdriver and removed another small panel on the bot's breast. She pulled out a little black semi-circle, about an inch wide, with a bundle of wires coming out the back. The black object was covered in dust. Gerti sat down on the floor next to them and watched.

"Eeeaaasy," she said, pointing at two frayed wires coming off the black object. She pulled the two damaged wires out of the bot's breast that matched the color of the other two wires. She popped her head up and looked around the apartment.

"Hey can you grab a rag and the soldering iron? And some solder - maybe the paste too. And the electrical tape? It's on the bench over there."

Gerti got up and retrieved all the items. She looked over at the couch and noted that Joe was sleeping. Hopefully he didn't have too bad of a concussion. Purcevale was standing on his hind legs, sniffing around Joe.

She gave the items to Gloria then got another rag, dampened it with some water, and put it on Joe's forehead. He didn't have a fever but she knew it would be nice for the headache.

Gloria and the bot had moved over by the wall where she could plug in the soldering iron. It took her a few minutes to reconnect them and apply insulation. Gerti watched her lay the tape over the wires longways and then wrap all five of them together. Purcevale sat curled up on Joseph's chest, judgmentally watching Gloria work.

"Eh, it's not pretty but it'll work," she said before going back to the service panel and pressing a few buttons.

The surface of the black semi-circle turned a shimmery orange. It emitted an orange light into the floor. Gloria humphed triumphantly and put the now-orange object back in the bot's breast.

The light it was displaying formed into a 3D model representing a section of the University campus. There were small humans moving around the grounds - hundreds of them running. Some of them were huddled in groups. A lot of them were running and hiding in the semi-transparent buildings.

"Whoa," they said in unison.

Gloria looked through the controls.

"That's the building where we met Joe." Gerti said. The dome on the building and the courtyard was hard to mistake.

"There's a list of files - I think they're memory files - but they're not labeled." Gloria pressed a button and the orange light transformed into a single room. It was small. Gerti recognized it as the dorm room where Gwen had taken her. Clothes were piled up all around the messy space.

"This is the first file." Gloria said. The holographic bot was laid out, disassembled, on David's bed. It twitched and looked up at him.

"Yes! Yes, yes, yes, yes! Hoooly shit, yes!" David exclaimed.

"'D'ya get it?" a figure on the other bed asked.

"Y-Yeah! I was right! And they were just gonna throw her away!" He patted the sides of the bare robot. The hologram skipped around after that. It showed David painting the 'V' on her side.

"Now you're sure about this? It'll be with you forever, you know? Have you thought about what this is going to look like in a hundred years - when you're old?" he asked, before chuckling to himself and continuing.

The hologram showed a few different times when professors had congratulated David for fixing such a complicated machine. He would beam and start patting the bot. The hologram shifted to an even smaller room than his dorm. Gerti recognized it as the supply closet they found the bot in. The holographic version of the bot was sitting next to a figure with its paws up on his chest.

"Hey - hey Bud, it's okay. You'll be okay." David said slowly. He held his chest with one hand and patted the side of the bot with the other.

"Who is that?" Gloria asked quietly, gently pointing at the figure. Her index finger phased through the light.

"A guy named David. He was a student before the fires."

The whole display rotated with Gloria's hand as she pulled it back. She did it again and the image focused on David's face. The detail was incredible - they could make out individual hairs on David's stubbly face and they could hear him struggling for breath. David chuckled.

"I guess nothing we did really matters now. Huh? Still proud of us though," he said, resting his head against the wall.

He shifted to lay down next to the bot and wrapped his arm around it. The surroundings of the closet faded away and the 3D display focused on David's chest. His heartbeat became louder and a jagged line, that corresponded to the sound, appeared on his chest. His heartbeat slowed until the line was flat.

The holographic bot whined and curled up next to David's body. The hologram became solely focused on what was happening in the closet. The outline of the small room was hard - nothing outside was being monitored. Gerti and Gloria watched as David's body quickly withered. The bot remained motionless. The details of the individual items in the room degraded until they were basic shapes. The door opened slowly. Gerti walked in and crouched next to them. The recording cut out when it snapped at her hand.

"Can you go to the most recent?" Gerti asked. Gloria selected another file and the hologram jumped to life again. It was the interior of Joe's apartment. Gerti and Gloria were both sitting next to the bot - their movements mirrored by the hologram. Gerti held up a hand and watched the small version of her copy with barely a delay. She reached down and zoomed in on the three of them. The detail was still nowhere near as good as it had been. Gerti and Gloria were both almost unrecognizable.

Gerti zoomed out as far as she could. The hologram reached quite aways from Joe's apartment. It just reached Gloria's a little ways to the north. The cafe, the office, and on the other side of that street. People glowed brighter and were solid, compared to the hollow outlines of the decrepit buildings.

"Oh," she breathed. This was what the bot wanted to show them.

"What?" Gloria asked.

"Last night. We can see everything that happened."

Chapter Thirteen
September 26th 2114
Bryan, Texas
Gertrude Alvarez

Gloria's eyes widened.

She returned to the service panel and clicked through the files. The buildings stayed the same but the people jumped around inside the hologram as it changed.

Everyone was in their homes lying in bed. Gloria pressed something and it jumped to mid-afternoon. The bot was with everyone in the cafe. She pressed the button again and the bot was back inside Joe's apartment - curled up next to the door. Gloria zoomed in on her apartment down the street.

She and Gwen were sitting around the coffee table talking. Gerti was walking down the street carrying Willow's rifle back to the hotel. That was based almost entirely off of context since the model detail was so low.

"Okay, so Jordan's watch must've just started." Gerti said. About an hour passed of nothing happening. Eventually the tiny Gwen laid down on the couch and Gloria went to her room for the night.

"This is really creepy." Gloria said.

"Yeah, I'm trying not to think about it. How's it gettin' all this anyway?"

"Magic, I guess."

"Right - of course." Gerti said, grinning.

A thin figure walked into the rendering and leaned against the cafe wall. They checked their watch a few times before another, burlier, figure joined them from the direction of the town hall and the parking garage. The two of them walked down the street to Gloria's apartment. Gloria zoomed in. They couldn't make out the details but, based on the builds, it looked like two men. The thin one raised a hand to stop the burly one from doing something. Then he stepped up and put the palm of his right hand on the door.

Gwen quickly sat up from her place on the couch before going limp and falling back down. The burly one pulled out a long, slender, object and placed it in the doorframe - the door swung open. The burly one briskly walked up to Gwen and scooped her up into his arms. They carried her down the street, heading south, and left the 3D render. A few minutes passed and Gloria woke up, got ready, and walked to Joe's to wake him up.

"How'd they get in? The door wasn't damaged." Gloria asked.

"Your door frame is loose. They probably bent it out a little so the door's lock would come out. I noticed it earlier today."

"We should show Joseph." Gloria said.

"He needs to sleep off his concussion."

"Who do you think those people are? What do they want with Gwen? Where were they taking her?" Gloria asked.

"I might know why they took her but I don't know the other two."

Gloria raised an eyebrow. Gerti debated whether or not to tell Gloria about Gwen being a mutant. She had seen the non-flattering poster about mutants.

"We should talk to Harold. I don't think he's the one that destroyed the batteries." Gerti said.

"Oh. No. He's a sweet guy. He wouldn't do something like that - especially not to just get Krystal's stuff from Lucas."

"Hey, can you play the files from earlier today. The bot took me and Joe to a building outside the walls. I want to see the inside." Gerti said.

Gloria found the files and started playing them. It ran through the events leading to finding the old police station. The insides of the building laid out before them - including the tigers inside.

"Ugh?" Gloria said when she noticed them.

"Tigers. The whole building's bricked up and the front doors are chained." She pointed to the windows that were rendering mostly solid. There appeared to be six adult tigers and seven cubs running around inside the building. There were several small rooms with figures lying motionless on beds. They zoomed in. The figures had a tube connecting both their arms to bags lying below the bed.

"She's a mutant." Gerti said. She pointed to the bags.

"Gwen?"

"I don't know what her deal is but yeah." Gerti said, nodding.

"She isn't from the north camp, is she? She said she was from the East Coast."

"What's the north camp?" Gerti asked.

"It's a group of mutants that attacked us a few years ago. She isn't with them, is she? She's too nice to be a mutant."

"I don't think she's with them."

A figure walked into the room they were zoomed into - it looked like the thin figure from the night before. He sat down in a chair next to the bed, crossed his legs, and laid a hand on the unconscious person's arm. He sat like that for a few minutes before patting the person's arm and standing. The rendering faded away as the trooper bot walked back to town.

"I knew something was up. Willow told me the town got so much money from trading but that didn't make sense." Gerti said.

"Wait, so they're bleeding mutants out? Do you think Willow knows about it?"

"In some capacity, I'd bet. That would explain her acting weird yesterday."

"But who are those other people?" Gloria asked.

Gerti shrugged. She walked over to Joe and grabbed the pistol holstered on his belt. She checked the chamber, clicked the safety on, then stuffed it in her beltline.

"One in the chamber with the safety off, huh?" Gerti asked under her breath. Joe didn't answer. She smiled and pulled her coat over the handgun.

"What's that for?" Gloria asked.

"We're gonna go talk to Willow. Close 'im up so he can come too. It'll be good to record anything that happens." She said, pointing to the bot.

Gloria nodded and put the side panel back in place.

"You're not going to hurt Willow, are you?"

"That's really up to her." Gerti left her rifle leaning against the wall as the two of them walked out of the apartment. She didn't want to have to maneuver around it if things went south. They climbed the ladder to the north watchtower where Willow was stationed. She looked back a little surprised to see them.

"What's up guys?" she asked.

"I have some questions for you." Gerti said.

"Oh yeah?" Willow asked, turning in her seat.

"Do you know what happened to Gwen?" Gerti asked.

Willow opened her mouth but Gerti cut her off before she could answer.

"And look - I know someone in town is harvestin' mutant blood for the crystals. I know two people broke into Gloria's apartment and took Gwen. I'm fairly certain the destroyed batteries are connected to Gwen and not the thing with Harold. I know she's being held in the old police station outside town and I know it's being guarded by tigers - so no bullshittin'."

Willow took a deep breath and considered her options - her face was tight.

"I can't," she said.

"You can't what?"

"Can't tell you anything. Please don't ask? Okay?"

"Willow? What's going on?" Gloria asked.

"If I tell y'all, Miguel'll die."

"Willow, I can help you - but you need to tell me what's happening." Gerti said.

Willow clenched her jaw and closed her eyes.

Gerti sat down in the vacant chair and reached out a hand to Willow's knee.

"I'm assuming if a bullet could've solved this it would already've been taken care of?" she asked.

Willow nodded.

"Fine." Willow sighed. "He's prolly already gonna have someone kill me anyway. Frank asked me to kidnap Gwen. I've done it before - well not kidnappin' but I've captured mutants in the wilds before. I said I didn't want to - he said that he was disappointed but that it was fine. 'He'd find someone else to do it and he'd find something else for me to do.' He probably made a deal with Lucas to get Harold arrested. I should be halfway to finding Miguel and just leavin' this place behind."

"What did he ask you to do? Instead of kidnappin' Gwen." Gerti asked.

"Nothing yet. I should've put a bullet in him right then but he wouldn't let me." Willow said.

"What do you mean? He wouldn't let you?" Gerti asked.

Gloria answered.

"He does that sometimes - you can feel it. It's like he's driving your brain. I thought I was imagining it."

Willow shook her head.

"I thought I was too when I first noticed it. But there are times when I'll think somethin' and he'll answer like I said it out loud." Willow said.

"Great, so let's kill him, from afar, and be done with it." Gerti said.

"We won't be able to. He can sense danger coming. I can't count the amount of times... There was one time he was walking out of his house and he stopped before walking through the door. He asked me to go out the back and check the hotel roof. Tanner Williams was up there with a rifle trained on the mayor's door."

"Wait, what happened to him?" Gloria asked.

"I killed him - he was trying to shoot the mayor. I was going to arrest him but he swung the rifle around at me. The mayor wanted to avoid anything public - that's why we said Tanner just left town."

Gloria pursed her lips.

"Did you ask how he knew?" Gerti asked.

"I was too scared." Willow said. "It really shook me up."

"What do you think's gonna happen to Harold?" Gloria asked.

"Frank'll prolly have Lucas go kill him - Or Jordan. Neither of 'em like him." Willow said.

"Well, let's go make sure he's okay - maybe even bust him out. We can figure out what to do about the mayor later." Gerti said.

Willow nodded.

"Jacob's watching the front door of the jail. He won't let us in."

"There's a door on the roof." Gloria said.

"Yeah, but we keep it locked." Willow said.

Gloria pulled a set of keys out of her pocket and found one. She looked at the teeth to confirm then held it up.

"That's troubling." Willow said. She stood up and grabbed her rifle.

Gerti climbed out of the tower and bent down next to the bot.

"I need you to go stay with Joe," she said.

The bot ran off towards Joe's apartment.

The three of them climbed the ladder on the side of the block of buildings and went across the roof to the office where Harold was being held. Gloria found the key and unlocked the roof door. They descended the building and Willow guided them to the offices being used as jails.

"I got this one." Willow said to Gloria, as she pulled a key out and slid it into the door. Harold was tied up in a chair in the corner of a dark office.

His head was leaning against the wall. Gerti checked the front door to make sure there wasn't a line of sight between it and the room. Satisfied, she clicked the light on. Harold's jaw was slacked open and the front of his body was covered in blood. There was blood sprayed to the sides on the wall behind him.

"Oh." Gerti breathed.

Willow cursed and Gloria left the room with her hands over her mouth.

"That son of a bitch." Willow said, marching towards the front door. She unlocked the door - Gerti could hear Jacob start to say something but Willow grabbed him and pulled him into the office.

"Jacob, what the hell happened?" she yelled.

"How'd y-"

"Shutchur damn mouth. What'd he give you?"

"What are you talking about?" Jacob asked.

Willow pushed him back into the wall.

"Hey, what's going on?"

"Who's been in here?" Willow asked.

"Lucas. He said he wanted to apologize to Harold. Jordan was on watch and went in with him. Willow, what's going on?" Realization swept across his face. He ran towards the hall where Harold was being kept. He started for a moment when he saw Gerti standing in the dark hallway watching. He shook it off and passed her. He stood in the doorway looking at the bloody scene.

"I'm gonna kill them," he said under his breath. "We need to get to Harold's."

The four of them sprinted across the town to the barbershop. The door to the upstairs apartment was locked. Jacob banged on the door. There was yelling inside. He kept banging on the door. Gloria pushed past him and unlocked it.

They barreled into the barber's apartment. Lucas and Krystal were standing on either side of a dining room table yelling - tears were streaming down Krystal's face. Lucas turned to the front door - his arms and torso were covered in drying blood and he had a red-stained crowbar in his hands.

"Lucas! Put the crowbar down." Jacob said, his rifle trained on Lucas' chest.

"Mind your business," he yelled.

"If you don't drop that crowbar, my business will be puttin' you down."

"Jacob, you're not in charge here. This is between me and her."

"I swear to God - I'll put a bullet through your head and sleep sound tonight."

"Fine." Lucas said, letting the crowbar drop to the floor. He raised his empty hands.

"Despite the evidence, I still feel the need to ask. Did you kill Harold?" Jacob asked.

"No Jake. He was alive when I left him." Lucas said.

"Okay. You didn't finish him off - but you put him on the brink of it?"

"What would you've done?" Lucas asked.

"Doesn't matter what I would've done. What'd you come here for?"

"I came to get Krystal - take her home where she belongs." Lucas said.

Gerti was standing near Krystal. She could see bruises forming on her wrists and one on the left side of her face. She looked at Jacob and saw that he had been looking at Krystal as well.

"Oh Lucas." Jacob breathed.

Two thunderous reports filled the apartment as he put two rounds through Lucas. He crumpled to the ground. Krystal screamed and everyone covered their ears. Gerti realized that at this point, she was going to have ringing in her ears for the rest of her life. Krystal sat down at the table and buried her head between her crossed arms. Willow and Gloria went and sat down next to her.

"I'm... sorry Krystal." Jacob said. He turned and saw Gerti looking at him.

"What?" he asked.

"Not a thing. What are you doin' about Jordan?" she asked.

"Depends on how he behaves." He passed Gerti and went down the stairs to the street - Gerti followed.

Jordan had climbed out of the south tower and was cautiously walking towards the barbershop. He stopped in his tracks when he saw Jacob and Gerti coming into the street. He unlooped his rifle strap from his shoulder and placed it on the ground. Then he raised his hands and backed up from his gun.

"You mind gettin' that?" Jacob asked.

Gerti retrieved the surrendered rifle. It was military from before the fires - the black finish was almost done wearing off the metal receiver. The fire-select only had two options - so maybe not a military rifle. She slung it over her shoulder like how Willow carried hers - it hung in front of her.

"What should I do with you?" Jacob asked.

Jordan opened his mouth to say something but must've had a hard time finding the right words.

"Go to Harold's cell." Jacob said.

"Need my help?" Gerti asked.

"No Ma'am. Thank you though." Jacob said, leading Jordan back to the jail offices at gunpoint.

People were poking their heads out their doors to watch the commotion. Gerti ducked out of the street and back up the stairs to Harold's apartment. Willow got up, quickly approached Gerti, and spoke under her breath.

"Hey, no gunshots. Jordan go quietly?" she asked.

Gerti nodded.

"How's she doin'?" Gerti asked, nodding at Krystal, who was crying into her arms while Gloria sat next to her. Her hand was on Krystal's back as she stared wide eyed at the table.

"I mean, not the best day but… she'll be better off. Hey, I need your help." Willow pointed at Lucas.

They made a stretcher from a sheet and two brooms and carried Lucas' body into another room so Krystal didn't have to look at him. The rounds had made a mess of his upper chest.

Willow took his boots off and set them aside. Out of curiosity, Gerti picked one up and looked at the rubber treads. She couldn't be sure, but they looked an awful lot like the ones outside the old police building.

"Does Jacob normally make these kinds of calls?" Gerti asked.

"No - but domestic abuse is a sore subject for him. He prolly would've done this a lot earlier if there'd been proof." Willow said.

They cleaned up the blood as well as they could. Someone entered the apartment. Gerti turned and saw that it was Frank. He was visibly dismayed at the sight of blood and at Krystal sobbing at the table.

"Jacob told me what happened. I am so sorry," he said, sitting down at the table and reaching a hand across. Krystal took his outstretched hand.

"He just... wanted... to help me." Krystal said through heaving breaths.

"Harold?" Frank asked.

She nodded and buried her face in her arms again.

"You're gonna be okay. None of this is your fault," he said, squeezing her hand.

"Harold would be alive if - " she began.

"You needed help because Lucas was mistreating you. Harold was a good man that chose to get involved. Lucas is the one that caused this. Not you. Okay?" Frank said.

"Okay." Krystal quietly agreed.

Gerti looked at the mayor's shoes.

They were brown leather cowboy boots. It would make sense if he had gone with Lucas to take Gwen into the police station. If what Gloria and Willow were saying was true, and he had weird abilities, then he could keep Gwen asleep and keep the tigers calm.

Shit. she thought, if it was true they needed to get away from him or he'd read their thoughts. On the other hand, perhaps it was too late and he had already heard everything.

"Gloria? Will you take Krystal to see Doctor Harrison?" Frank asked.

Gloria nodded and helped Krystal stand up. Together, they walked out of the apartment. Frank shifted in the dining room chair so that he was facing Gerti and Willow who were still wiping up the pool of blood in the middle of the room.

"Gertrude, do you mind stepping out? I need to speak with Willow," he asked.

Her body stood to leave but Willow grabbed her hand and pulled her back. Gerti tried to galvanize herself against being manipulated but it had happened so naturally and quickly. With Willow anchoring her, she stayed.

"Okay. I owe apologies to both of you anyway. Willow, let's start with you. I was reflecting on our conversation the other day and I think I may have not been as clear as I could've been - should have been. My comment about Miguel had nothing to do with what I was asking of you. I was genuinely giving my hopes for a safe journey and noting that the wasteland was dangerous while encouraging you by saying he is perfectly capable of surviving in it. There was no veiled threat - I would never do that to you. You've stood by me through so much. If you have questions, please ask them." He looked at her, waiting for questions.

Willow didn't speak.

Frank smiled warmly. It set Gerti's teeth on edge.

"Yes, but please ask them aloud so she can hear them too," he said, nodding at Gerti.

"Did you make a deal with Lucas to have Harold arrested?" Willow asked.

"Yes." Frank said, his smile fading.

"So he would kidnap Gwen?" Gerti asked.

"Yes. I never meant for any of this to happen though. Harold was a prince among men," he answered.

"Which also brings me to your apology. Ms. Alvarez, -"

"Get out of my head." Gerti said quickly. She hadn't told anybody her last name and she'd swear she could feel him rooting around.

"Sorry - it's second nature at this point. Can I go on?" he asked.

"If you stay out of my head," she replied.

He nodded.

218

"I apologize for taking Gwen. But I can't let her go, and even if I could, she wouldn't want to leave. She's the happiest she's been in her entire life."

"What do you mean?" Gerti asked.

"She's in a paradise of her own mind - anything she wants. Do you know what she's doing right now? She's teaching her father how to play poker. They're sitting and enjoying each other's company for the first time in almost ten years. Isn't that beautiful? Would you take that away from her?" he asked.

"Have you given her a choice to leave?" Gerti asked.

"Not in so many words but why would I - she's happy. Would you like to feel how happy she is?"

He closed his eyes and a wave of nostalgia washed over Gerti - nostalgia for a time and place she had never experienced. She focused on the smell of gunsmoke and blood to pull herself back into the apartment.

"It's not real. Just something you're making for her," she said.

"Technically, she's making it for herself. Regardless, why are you trying so hard to pull that poor girl back into this grim reality? You hardly know her. Did you know she can do what I can do? What if she's been manipulatin' you into helpin' her - takin' her in?"

"Has she?" Gerti asked.

"I've no way of knowin'. Could be." Frank said with a shrug.

"Hasn't felt like it. What are you goin' to do if I decide to go to the old police station, kill your tigers, and get her - along with the other mutants you're holdin'?" Gerti asked.

"How'd you - nevermind. Listen, the other mutants were bandits. Keepin' 'em was kinder than just killin' 'em."

"That's not true." Willow said, "Some of them were just travelers we ambushed."

"Well yes, but they were still monsters - bandits, thugs, marauders, just like all the mutants we've come across."

"Gwen's not a monster." Gerti said.

"She was able to take a shot from an energy rifle and keep truckin'. She killed her father when she was a child and, conveniently, can't remember anything about her life?"

"We all have blood on our hands. That doesn't mean she's a monster." Willow said.

"Maybe that's wishful thinking on your part," he said.

"Mkay - 'nough of this bullshit." Gerti said.

She pulled Joe's pistol out of her belt, aimed it at the mayor's torso and pulled the trigger. Well, she tried to pull the trigger but it was stuck. She looked at the pistol - the trigger had rusted into a solid piece with the frame and wouldn't budge.

"You'd think Joseph, of all people, would take better care of his firearms." Frank said.

There was a metallic click from behind Gerti. She tried to turn her head to look but her muscles were stiff and she wasn't able. She saw out of the corner of her eye that Willow had pulled Lucas' revolver and primed the hammer. It was aimed at Frank but her arm was frozen and her eyes were wide - filled with terror.

"I'm sorry girls. This has gotten out of hand. I'm goin' to give y'all some time to consider what you're doin'." Frank said. He turned around and left the apartment but popped his head back in.

"I'll go talk to Pastor, we'll have a service for Harold tonight - probably bury Lucas in the mornin' if y'all want to be there for that." He gently patted the doorframe and walked out again.

They heard him saying goodbye to Krystal who was outside on the landing. A few minutes passed before Gerti could feel her muscles again. Willow let out a deep breath and started patting herself down.

"You okay?" Gerti asked.

"Did you see that too or was it just in my head?" Willow asked.

"I didn't see anything. My gun just jammed." Gerti looked at the pistol's trigger - it was clean. She cleared the chamber and pulled the trigger a few times.

Everything was working properly. She loaded a fresh round into the chamber and put it back in her belt.

"His face was just wrong - it was all movin' around. I couldn't move - I don't know. Let's just get outta here," she said. Krystal was sitting on the steps of the apartment.

"You gonna be alright, Krys'?" Willow asked.

She looked up and nodded.

Willow handed Lucas' revolver to her. Gerti and Willow walked down into the street. The mayor was nowhere to be seen. Gloria and Dr Harrison walked past them - Gloria pointed him up the stairs then came back to Gerti and Willow. The three of them walked up to Joe's apartment and sat down around his living room and talked about the conversation with the mayor.

Joe woke up during the conversation and was caught up. He and Gloria were disappointed and terrified to hear all this about the mayor. Frank took Gloria under his wing when she left her folk's farm a few years ago and Joe had worked for him since he was fifteen. Neither one of them had ever really seen this side of him.

"If we go together, we'll be able to get through the tigers - there are only thirteen." Gerti said.

"Oh. Only thirteen." Joe repeated.

"There's four of us and we're all armed." Willow said.

"What about guard duty? Jordan's locked up and Jacob's watching him. That pretty much just leaves you two." Gloria said, pointing at Gerti and Willow.

"You can go get Allen to split the two watchtowers." Willow said.

"The hell? I'm going with y'all." Gloria replied.

"Okay, then we'll have to roll the dice on nothin' happenin' while we're gone." Willow said.

Gerti pulled Joe's pistol out and handed it back to him. He checked it over and put it back in its holster without saying anything.

"How're you feeling?" she asked.

"Good enough," he answered, then chuckled after a second. "Good enough," he repeated. Gerti tilted her head and raised an eyebrow, wondering what was funny.

"We were talking about tiger prison guards the other day. What are the odds?" he asked.

She smiled.

Chapter Fourteen
September 26th 2114
Southbound Highway 6
Brandon Clements

Brandon Clements laid beneath the metal carcasses of scorched cars on a burned out and cracked highway. The sun had gone down several hours ago and the wind was getting cold. There was a pile of concrete rubble and loose rocks piled up along the hulls of the vehicles that blocked the wind from biting at him.

He had thought about going to Bryan but that seemed like a bad idea. That left the mutant colony to the north - again, not the best idea, and the Fairegrounds. That's where he was heading now.

After leaving the University, he had gone south on the old highway before taking an eastern turn onto an intersecting highway. There had been a smattering of buildings and rust-worn machines lining the side of the road - several old concrete overpasses had collapsed.

He had heard about the Fairegrounds people and he knew they were odd but he figured they could use someone with medical training. That, and they were the only other group he knew about that were friendly to outsiders. He pulled his blanket up over his shoulders.

Suddenly, a harsh white light came from the sky and illuminated his section of highway. With it was a small whirring noise - like an old fan or a broken piece of technology. The car kept him from the light.

It slowly hovered over the road to the south. Brandon clutched the handle of his mentor's revolver and turned his head to follow the light. There were three massive figures standing in the open road. They were muscled, covered in long black hair, and had clearly been moving towards Brandon's shelter.

One stood to its full height and sheltered its eyes against the light. It was impressively tall.

Brandon froze in fear.

Two mechanical figures slowly descended from the skies.

They each had large backpacks with a section coming out the bottom that looked like thick tails. The hairy creatures, probably mutants of some kind, bared their teeth and let out a guttural growl. They were probably fifty feet away but he could still see their dog-like maws filled with rows of sharp, stained, fangs.

The two mechanical figures raised weapons.

225

The hairy creatures charged and all three were smoothly put down with well placed bolts of blue energy.

The figures crumpled onto the ground - thick plumes of smoke raised from their singed fur.

The mechanical figures scanned the area before one of them took their helmet off. Their heads were elongated and covered in green scales. It lifted its head to the sky and took in a deep breath. It said something to its companion in a low gravelly voice. It was in a language Brandon didn't understand.

The other one smacked him on the arm and said something back that sounded like chastising. The first one put its helmet back on and bent down next to the bodies.

It placed something on each hairy body - they began to hover about three feet off the ground. The two figures began guiding the corpses to where they had descended but their attention snapped to yelling that came from the southern side of the highway.

Brandon looked. A group of muscle-bound men wielding all manner of ancient melee weapons burst onto the road. The man in the lead was wearing a loose long-sleeved shirt, a plaid skirt, and red tennis shoes. He hefted a massive two-handed sword over his head and swung it around at the two suited figures.

The backpacks disintegrated - revealing large leathery wings. They took off towards the sky with a few powerful wingbeats. Brandon's mouth hung open. What the hell kind of mutant was that?

The massive sword landed on vacated air. Brandon inched over until he could see the flying figures. They halted in the bright beam of light, like they had been caught by an invisible net, and began ascending in the same manner they had arrived.

The bodies of the three hairy creatures followed them into the sky.

The leader of the attackers, dropped his sword, jumped onto one of the floating creatures, and began cutting at the fur with a knife - yelling the entire time. He must have removed whatever device the winged mutants had attached, because the creature and the man fell from the sky - about twenty feet to the ground. He landed on his hands and knees. One of the other men helped him up. Another handed him his discarded sword. They all laughed and high-fived each other as the light began to move away. It veered off and the whirring noise disappeared into the night.

Brandon could hear the men talking. One of them sparked a fire. In the dim light, Brandon could see the leader skinning the hairy creature and draining its blood into a catch bucket. He placed the creature's torso on a block of broken highway before taking his sword and removing the dog-like head.

"Glory to the Gee-Em!" he yelled in a raspy voice, while holding the severed head aloft.

The men with him, probably a dozen, repeated the phrase. One of the men approached the leader. He was wearing a loose-fitting robe with something tied around his waist.

"Did you get the device?" he asked.

"I'm sorry, Francis. It pulled loose from my grasp," he replied.

The other men gathered around the body and allowed the leader to pour blood from the bucket into vessels they produced. Once they were finished, the leader stepped onto the shell of a destroyed car and lifted the mug he was holding.

"To the men on hiiiigh," he said reverently, letting the long 'I' fade.

"Let the crimson silver flow," the other men said in unison.

"To the warriors tried," he said.

"Let the spoils go," the others finished.

They put the vessels to their lips and drained them.

"Thank you, fiend," the leader said quietly to the dead creature.

Two of the men dismembered the creature and cooked parts of it over the fire. They sat in a circle around the flames eating in silence.

Finally, one of them asked if they should camp there for the night or head back to the castle. These people had to be from the Fairegrounds. The leader took in a deep breath and let out a guttural sigh.

"Let's go home, brothers. Before the great beast catches our manly scent." The others laughed with their leader. They lit torches off their fire before putting it out.

Brandon took a deep breath and slid out from under the cars.

"Howdy!" he called, in his friendliest voice.

The men turned their bodies to face Brandon - one of them pulled a bow off his shoulder and nocked an arrow.

"What is your name, stranger?" the leader asked.

"Brandon. Clements. I'm from the university just north of here. I'm looking for the Fairegrounds. Are y'all with them?" Brandon tried to keep his voice steady but he knew he was failing. If this went south, he only had six rounds on standby.

"Yes. What do you want there?" he asked.

"I'm a medic. I'm just looking for somewhere to help."

"Are you alone?" he asked.

"Yes." Brandon answered tentatively.

"Francis, help him gather his things. The Gee-Em will find a place for a white-mage."

The man in the brown robe approached Brandon. He held a torch in his right hand and showed his left hand to be empty. Brandon rolled up his blanket and tied it to the outside of his backpack.

"It's okay, this is everything." he said.

Francis nodded and walked him back to the group.

"Swane the pain train," the leader said, holding out a hand.

"Pardon?" he asked, shaking the massive calloused hand.

"My name is Swane the pain train." Each long A was more drawn out than it should have been.

"Is 'The Pain Train' part of your name or is it a title?" Brandon asked cautiously.

"Pain isn't just my name, brother - it's my calling. I am the hammer that breaks the wicked, the storm that topples the tyrant! The Pain Train runs at full steam, and I ain't stoppin' 'til the tracks give out. Oh yeah." Swane replied, looking out into the middle distance.

"It's both." Francis said to Brandon.

"It's all three." Swane corrected.

They walked for about twenty minutes before coming to a concrete overpass - parts of it were crumbling off. Francis and Brandon were towards the back of the group as they walked. Brandon could see the cord tied around Francis' waist was an old power cable that was wrapped around several times before meeting in a knot at his front.

"What were those things?" Brandon asked.

"Which ones?" he asked.

"Either."

"The hairy creatures are cursed men - our texts refer to them as werewolves or dogmen. Sometimes it's hard to make the texts line up perfectly with our new world but in this case it lines up pretty well." Francis replied.

"They're mutants? Why did y'all drink their blood?"

"They did - I didn't. It's part of their battle rituals. It's forbidden for my order. The werewolves were products of the fires if that's what you mean by mutant." Francis said.

"Does their blood crystalize like other mutants?" Brandon asked.

Francis nodded.

"What about the other things?" Brandon asked.

"We don't know - demons maybe. The Gee-Em says he thinks they're part of the race that used to rule the Earth." Francis said.

Brandon let this sit for a moment.

"I've never heard about them," he finally said.

"The Gee-Em believes a great many things without tangible evidence. Does your group deal with mutants often?" Francis asked.

"Fortunately, no. The Trustee Bots have kept them out."

"How do you guide the machines? We've lost a lot of acolytes to them over the years." Francis said.

"I'm sorry to hear that. We don't control them - nobody does anymore. They've just been running off very old programming. I'm surprised y'all would let me join you - if you thought we were controlling the bots."

Francis turned to Brandon and shrugged. He had a young face - couldn't have been much older than sixteen.

"What's your role?" Brandon asked.

"I'm looking for technology to bring back to the scholars. It's the next step in my advancement," he answered.

The road they were walking down was in the bottom of a shallow valley like most old highways. Brandon felt like they were too exposed but none of the other men seemed worried and he felt like he was better equipped than them. He didn't relax though - every part of his body was uncomfortable right now. He missed his dorm and he missed the other cadets.

The group came to another highway intersection with a fallen overpass. Swane stopped and signaled for everyone to follow suit. He sniffed the air.

"I smell her," he said, filling his lungs with another deep breath through his nose. "Extinguish and hide - there," he said, pointing at the rubble of the overpass.

The group of strange people ran to the rubble and put out their torches. They found a large chunk of solid concrete that had fallen and created a large enough recess for all of them to hide underneath.

"What is it?" Brandon asked Francis. He began to answer but was cut off by Swane.

"A metal dragon stalks these skies," he said.

Several of the men reached into pouches on their plaid skirts and removed something shiny and square. They unfolded the objects into large metal sheets that crinkled loudly in the wind. They stepped up and one of them offered a corner of the thin metal blanket to Brandon.

"Hold this up to the opening. We need to hide from -"

Swane interrupted the man.

"The beast's vision sees only shades of fire. And it stays in the sky out of fear. Fear of us! It knows that if it lands it will have to face our steel and our wrath," he said, looking into his group.

They cheered quietly.

Brandon didn't know if they were riled up or trying to appease their leader.

"Heat. It sees heat." Francis said to Brandon.

Swane sighed tiredly at the clarification.

Brandon didn't know what a dragon was but he didn't want to find out. He held the blanket up to the corner of the concrete so it covered the opening. A low rumbling filled the air. Brandon was straining and could only barely hear it.

Then, through a small gap between the concrete and the blanket, he saw two cones of blue fire leading into the sky. It was hard to tell exact distances in the darkness, but further up from the cones, were two pin pricks of red light. The cones cut out but Brandon followed the red lights as they surveyed the area. He felt someone pulling at his shirt sleeve. It was Francis.

"Don't expose yourself," he said.

Brandon nodded and stayed behind the blanket.

They waited for what felt like forever but was probably no more than twenty minutes. Every once in a while Swane would take a deep breath and tell them to wait longer. Eventually, he said the coast was clear. The two men folded the blanket up and stowed them back in their skirt pouches.

"What's a dragon?" Brandon asked.

Swane looked at him like he was stupid.

"The zenith of our forefather's hubris," he replied.

Brandon decided he would ask Francis about it later so he could get a straight answer.

The group walked for several more hours, in silence, before turning off the road to cross a field. In the distance, Brandon could see points of firelight spaced out on a stone wall. As they got closer, he could see that the walls were about fifteen feet tall and were made from chunks of broken up concrete. Two large metal doors split the wall and there was a collapsible ladder attached horizontally to the top or the doorway. A man with a pointed metal helmet came to the edge.

"Hail heir," the man called down.

"Aye! Hail heir, Brother." Swane said back.

The man rolled his hand like he was waiting for something.

"I'm tired, Gulliver," Swane said, sighing.

"It's Gee-Em's orders. In case of changelings." Gulliver said with a smile.

"I know it's just orders. Vitsaar Tartivum." Swane said.

Mist began to flood the area. Blue glowing mist.

Brandon recoiled and tried to shake the mist off. He was incredibly dismayed to find out that the mist was coming from him - coming from each person. It emanated from his skin and faded out as it moved away from him.

"Wha-" he began to ask but trailed off.

The mist faded away entirely.

"Thanks Swane." Gulliver said.

He untied one end of the ladder and let it swing down to Swane, who caught it silently.

* * *

The four of them, and the Trooper, marched through the unguarded south gate after stopping to pick up Lucas' bloody crowbar. Krystal looked at them

235

confused when they walked into Harold's apartment but didn't ask what they were up to. Gerti had given Jordan's rifle to Gloria - Willow made sure she knew how to use it - and Joe had gotten his pump shotgun. They stopped in front of the building.

"Trooper, can you show what's inside the building right now?" Gerti asked.

The bot yipped.

A holographic version of the building displayed out the front of its breast. They saw themselves standing outside the building. Inside, they saw the group of tigers spread out in various piles asleep.

Downstairs, they could make out four mutants lying motionless on wall beds - one to a cell. Another room showed Gwen lying on the same style bed. A figure stood next to her with his hand resting on the side of her leg.

"Hey, that's pretty cool." Joe said.

The bot yipped again and wagged its tail.

"Yeah, the tigers are together. Easy." Willow said, calmly clicking the fire select on her rifle to auto.

"They'll probably wake up when we break the lock." Gerti said.

"We'll keep an eye on 'em." Willow said, pointing to the hologram.

Joe wedged Lucas' crowbar into the arch of the padlock and began prying. After a minute, Gerti helped and they broke the lock off the door.

They jumped back away from the entrance - Willow and Gloria had their rifles trained on the opening. After a few seconds of silence, they looked down at the hologram and saw the tigers still peacefully dozing.

All of them exchanged concerned looks, gritted their teeth, and entered the building. The old police station was littered in torn cloth and tiger excrement - the smell was overwhelming. They stopped for a moment to listen to the light chuffs of the tigers snoring.

"Aww." Gloria breathed under her breath.

The light emitting from the hologram cast a warm glow onto the otherwise ransacked and crumbling building. Joe kept an eye on the figures in the basement as they moved along. The trooper led them to a stairwell leading down - they moved down the stairs as quietly as they could.

The figure in the hologram dropped their hand from the figure in the bed and moved towards the hallway that the door would open into. Joe breathed a quiet curse and pointed to the hologram but everyone was already looking at it.

Gerti made a motion for everyone to cover their ears. She aimed her rifle at the door, estimating where the figure was based on the hologram. They heard muffled gunshots from outside. The door in front of them swung open. The mayor came face to face with the end of Gerti's rifle.

"Wait, before we do anything crazy-" he started.

Gerti rammed the barrel of her gun into his face like a spear. He howled and reeled back in pain, blood starting to pour from his cheek where the rifle had made contact.

"I'm keeping the tigers asleep! If I die they'll rip you all apart!" he shouted through his hands clasped to his face.

"You stay focused on that. Try to do anything else and we'll be taking our chances with the tigers." Willow said. Her rifle was trained on his chest.

More gunshots from outside - girthy, large caliber, semi-auto.

"Will someone *please* check that?" the mayor asked.

Gloria bent down beside the trooper bot and asked it to expand its view to the surface. A large group of people, around thirty, were in cover behind car hulls taking shots at the town wall. A single figure stood in the back pointing out targets. From his body language it looked like he was yelling orders.

"Cadets?" Joe asked.

"We can take 'em." Willow said.

"There're a lot of 'em." Gloria said.

"I can tell them to leave - or talk - or something." The mayor's voice was muffled behind his blood-soaked hands. "Please. For my family. For everyone in town. Let me take care of this and then we can talk."

238

Automatic fire joined the conversation outside. Two of the holographic cadets hit the ground. The shots picked up even more in response.

Joe broke first - someone had to.

"I say we let him."

"What if he tells the cadets to kill us." Willow said.

"I won't. Just shoot me if it looks that way." Frank muttered.

After a short pause, Gerti and Willow lowered their rifles. Together, they raced up the stairs and out the front doors - the mayor leading the way. Gerti barred the door behind them as they exited the police station. When they got outside, they could see the cadets slowly advancing on the town.

Several gunmen from the town were mounting a sparse defense. Danny was one of them. Two cadets, about forty feet away, turned and leveled their rifles at the group. They both fell unconscious to the ground at the mayor's silent command. The man issuing orders to the cadets turned. He was older than the rifle toters but Gerti didn't recognize him from the fight at the university.

"Stop this!" the mayor yelled.

The cadets lowered their rifles. The man in charge raised a pistol in his right hand but didn't fire. The mayor and Willow slowly approached the cadets. The rest stayed behind and got close to the piles of concrete and broken down cars that surrounded the south gate - in case they needed to dive for cover. Willow and Mayor's pace slowed about fifty feet from the rest of the group. A handful of the cadets, and their leader, met them there.

Gerti had a bad feeling in the pit of her stomach. She moved to a pile of rubbish and laid down behind it, resting her rifle in the crook of a bent piece of rebar. She put her iron sights on the mayor's back.

Joe watched Gerti do this.

Words were exchanged between the mayor and the cadet's leader but they couldn't hear what was being said.

"Hey Willow!" Joe motioned for her to come back.

She nodded and started moving back to them.

Gerti couldn't hear any of the conversation happening. She saw the mayor nodding his head thoughtfully and looking off to the distance as he talked to their leader.

Her finger took the slack out of the trigger - expecting him to run at any moment. Gerti took a second to reflect on how the hell she managed to get in this situation and wished she could just duck out of the whole thing. Was that her thought or the mayor's?

She wasn't able to tell.

Chapter Fifteen
September 24th 2114
Bryan, Texas

"Checkmate," the girl said to her father again.

He smiled amiably and began resetting the pieces on the board. The smile still looked wrong on his ragged and grizzled face.

Growing up high on the east coast meant winters were hard for them and food was always scarce - everyday was a struggle and that had been reflected on her father's face in life. Even now in this dream-like state, his face was just as scarred as hers but for some reason they didn't seem as ghastly as they had before.

It had just been the two of them for some time. The younger version of herself had faded away as she became more comfortable with this new imaginary father figure before her. He was imaginary, right?

She began to reset her white pieces. When she was done she spun the board to let her father start. Another quick game passed with her winning.

His eyes were too happy to really be him. Board spin. Another game and another easy win. She was black this time but she decided to go first anyway. Her father didn't react and continued playing as normal. Another victory. Pieces reset. She reached across the board and knocked over her father's king.

"Checkmate."

He chuckled and smiled as he set the king back up and spun the board around for another game. His eyes were still bright and happy to be there - they were still wrong.

She looked around at their surroundings and noticed they were sitting in Mrs. Laredo's cafe. She jumped as a loud bang on the table caused chess pieces to fly onto the ground - the cafe disappeared and the blank surroundings overwhelmed her.

She snapped her head towards the noise to see her father's fist resting on the table where he had slammed it. His rugged face was wearing an expression more familiar to her. This wasn't right.

* * *

Something was wrong.

242

The mayor looked around and Gerti could tell he was worried about something. He turned back around and shook the cadet's leader's hand in an almost dismissive manner.

The cadets turned and left en masse without any more gunfire - the two who had fallen asleep awoke and moved groggily with their companions. The mayor turned heel and returned to the waiting group with a pained expression on his face.

Gerti let slack back into her trigger as Allen and Jacob drew up to them with rifles in hand. Their eyes widened in horror when they saw the blood on the mayor's face begin to crystalize into the telltale beads of a mutant.

He wiped it away, but it was too late.

* * *

"You're afraid of me," the girl said to her father who was steadily becoming more enraged.

"Of course I am!" he shouted. Except it wasn't his voice that came out. It was the other one from before. There was a smell of something musty in the air. Something pinching her arms in the crooks of her elbows.

"What am I doing?" she asked herself.

243

"You're living your dream, Sweetheart. Just spending time with your parents who adore you." a woman behind her said sweetly.

The girl turned to look at the woman - it was her mom. She relaxed for a moment until a crippling dart of fear shot up her spine.

No. No no no. She didn't know what her mom looked like. And where were they? In a theater? on the shores of the Gulf? In the courtyard of a gray stoned castle adorned with red and black banners? The cafe in Bryan?

"Look at me!" snapped the woman. It definitely wasn't her mom who the hell was it? Pieces fell into place. It was Mrs. Laredo with her Dad's scars on her face. Something broke in her mind's eye and the world surrounding them faded away - not to a blank void like before but to a darkened room where she was laid out on a table with a cracked leather cushion underneath her.

* * *

Gerti laid in her position, maybe fifty feet away from the mayor. Everyone else ran to him.

"Frank, are you -" Allen began, motioning to the crystalizing blood on the mayor's face.

"Listen to me. I need you two to go back inside the walls and make sure everyone stays in their homes. The situation is dealt with." Frank said.

"Okay, we can do that. But your face…" Jacob said, staring at the bead forming on the mayor's cheek.

"Do as I said, now."

As if turned by an invisible hand, the two men did what they were told without another word otherwise. Once they were through the gate, Frank turned to Joe, Gloria, Willow, and Gerti.

"I'll allow the girl to leave with Gertrude if y'all three agree to keep the peace and keep quiet. And the other mutants remain under my care. We have a good thing goin' here and I'm not going to let any of you interrupt that but I also don't want any more bloodshed today," he said.

"I do." Willow said, snapping the muzzle of her rifle into place inches from the side of his head.

"That's cute, but I'm being serious."

Willow's index finger was white from the pressure she was trying to exert on her rifle's trigger.

Joe stepped forward.

"How about this, you let all the mutants go and we leave town. Willow, Miguel, Gloria, and I can leave. You won't have to worry about us."

"I'd be losing two of my repair team and two of my security team. Not to mention a near limitless supply of crystal from the mutants. Besides, what bargaining power, let alone actual power, do you think you have right now?" he asked, grinning.

"I've always respected you for the work you put into this town - for the care you showed towards everyone." Joe began. "After my brother died, I didn't know what I was going to do with my life but you offered me a job and gave me a home where I could remember him with my work every day. And Gloria - you took her in when she left her parents. I think you're a good person, I wouldn't't've stayed here for so long if I thought otherwise. This," he motioned to the police station and the mutants within, "This was a mistake, a horrible mistake, but it's not too late to do better. Do the right thing, let them go - let us go. Even if you keep the crystal you already have. The town'll be okay."

"Well, I appreciate all that but it's not gonna happen, Joseph. I can tell you what will happen though. Gertrude and the girl will leave and I'll up the pay for the three of you to join me, in earnest." After a few seconds he added, "And you can drop the idea of freeing the mutants after you join me. I think I'm being more than reasonable."

"I won't be able to stand by this" Joe said.

"Why do you care, they're not even people for God's sake!"

"You're one of 'em!" Gloria yelled.

"Do you see a scorpion tail? Or dog legs!" The mayor reached down and slapped his boots. He took a deep breath, "I'm not a mutant, I have a gift. And I'm done with this conversation. Willow, be a dear and shoot them."

Tears rolled out of Willow's eyes as she swept her rifle to Joe.

A shot rang out in the otherwise silent world.

* * *

The darkness of her room was cut by a small lamp angled harshly onto the service of a dilapidated white desk in the corner. The girl slowly pivoted off the table she was on. Something sharp tugged at her arms that made her yelp.

Red tubes were attached to her arms with bands. She ripped them out. Small spurts of blood arced from the exposed needles. She took a deep breath and anger filled her lungs. As she stormed out of the room into the dark hallway outside, she felt more mutants in the rooms surrounding her. She peered in.

Mutants of various shapes and sizes were strapped to beds and hooked up to similar blood-filled tubes. One had the legs of a dog instead of human legs.

"I'm gonna rip him apart," she said under her breath. Frank had done this to them and he would pay.

There was a muffled gunshot from outside. She rushed towards the exit, up a flight of stairs, and into the tiger's den. All of the tigers awoke and looked at her as she ran into the room. She started for a moment as they got up and moved towards her. She furrowed her brow and kept eye contact with the one in front as she side-stepped towards the front door.

She carefully moved into the glass ante-chamber that separated the front door from the rest of the lobby. She tried to open the door but it didn't budge. As if sensing this, the tigers started running towards her.

The girl reached for the cross-bar door to the ante-chamber and pulled it shut. The beasts pawed at the door and prowled on the other side of it as they watched her. She looked around for something to bar the door with - a crowbar laid discarded on the floor.

She wedged it between the bar and the door frame before turning her attention to the front door again. There were more gunshots from outside. She looked through a small hole in the front door and saw muzzle flashes in the distance as more shots rang out in the twilight.

* * *

Willow yelled out and fell to the ground. Her rifle clattered beside her, a hole ran through her rifle's receiver. Metal blossomed out of the side. Gerti racked the bolt to load another round before moving it back to the mayor. She was three quarters of the way towards pulling the trigger when the trooper bot blocked her vision.

It was running at the mayor at an unimaginable speed.

The mayor commanded it to stop but the bot ignored him. It hit him in the chest like a bullet, knocking him to the ground.

The mayor pulled a pistol and fired into the bot's torso. He stood, blood now spreading on his white shirt, and pointed the pistol at the nearest person, Joe.

Everybody scrambled to do something. Gertrude stood to get a better shot on the mayor. Willow, still prone, pulled a long knife and darted towards the mayor.

Joe and Gloria were bringing their weapons to bear. Gertude had her irons on him but wasn't able to pull the trigger. Her eyes moved between the rest of her party and noticed they were similarly frozen in place and struggling, except the trooper bot. Its metal body clashed loudly on the concrete ground as it spasmed and writhed violently.

Irritated, the mayor aimed at the bot. Two more gunshots and it stopped moving. Gertrude wanted nothing more, in that moment, then to be able to pull the trigger as the mayor moved his weapon back to Joe.

* * *

The girl saw a figure stand up. She couldn't call any details about the figure but she knew it was Gerti. She was struggling with something. The girl walked through the locked door and ran to her friend. The world around her took on a soft lambent quality. At first, she thought it was due to the sunset but she realized it was something else. She saw everyone else frozen in place.

The mayor's arm was outstretched at Joe and the trooper bot was laying on the ground motionless.

"I can't!" Gerti cried.

The girl looked at her and saw that her mouth wasn't moving.

"What happened, what's wrong?" the girl asked.

"I can't pull the trigger. He won't let me." Gerti explained.

The girl got close.

"Are you on him?" she asked.

"Shoulder. Close enough." Gerti responded.

The girl placed her hand on top of Gerti's gun hand and cupped her trigger finger.

Together, they pulled.

* * *

Red mist and chunks of viscera erupted from the mayor's shoulder. The force of the bullet spun him around before he collapsed on the ground. Writhing, clutching his dangling arm, he began to crawl away.

Gerti turned to thank Gwen but she wasn't there. When she turned back to the mayor, Willow was on top of him driving her knife into his chest repeatedly. Gerti took off towards the police station to get Gwen.

Joe whipped around to make sure everyone was okay, then he ran to the bot and picked up its limp frame. Two bullets had ripped through the holographic display unit and distended parts of the neck. One shattered a connection point to the bot's mandible and the fourth bullet had broken one of the top exhaust ports off.

"You don't like being even, huh?" he asked. "Go to sleep. I'll get you going again."

The bot yipped weakly and powered down.

Chapter Sixteen
October 14th, 2114
Bryan Texas
Joseph Marion

After the mayor's death, Allen and Jacob stepped up into his place. Upon learning of the mutants, Allen freed them and offered them a place in the town.

Understandably, they declined and decided to head north to the mutant camp. It had been a solemn few weeks since then. Frank's family tried to leave town out of disgrace, but it was obvious to everyone they didn't know what he had been doing. So they were asked to stay. Joe figured the geniality was due to nobody in town being directly on the receiving end of the mayor's more severe abuses.

Miguel and his caravan returned safely.

The four of them talked about returning to the shelter but decided on staying in the town to help in the mayor's absence. Without the constant crystal supply they were all going to have to try harder to survive. The discussion of shuttering the town completely was also had but the general consensus was that they would try to make it first.

Gloria and Allen had made contact with the cadets and made a peace deal. They pinned the 'attack' on the dead mayor and that seemed to smooth a lot over with the group.

The tigers still lived in the police station and stalked the walls from time to time. They mostly left the townspeople alone though.

Gerti and Gwen left town the morning after everything happened. Joe wondered about them every day. He also wondered about the cadet who had helped them and wished he had offered him a place in Bryan.

"Shift's up." Miguel said as he climbed into the northern watch tower.

"Thanks, man." Joe replied. He climbed down and walked home to continue working on the trooper bot.

He passed the medic Trustee-Bot. Joe had gotten it up and running - recalibrating the friend or foe detection to be less hostile. It plodded down the street on its internal street patrol. He turned around to watch it walk off. Its white carapace body panels glistened in the light of the full moon. He was pretty proud of getting that one running right.

* * *

Brandon Clements was sitting on the bench next to a faux stone facade waiting to hear from Francis. It was getting dark and the full moon was coming over the burnt and splintered tree covered horizon.

He was waiting to hear if the Gee-Em and the Elder of the order would let him join Francis' order. Brandon thought that would be the best place for him. Everyone in the fairgrounds adhered to a fantastical view of the world that Brandon didn't think he would fit into. Although, the form to fit into this group seemed pretty wide.

There was Talon, a guy who seemed to be more machine than man. A slew of mutants who all smiled at Brandon when they passed him. There were even mutants that seemed more 'normal' like Swane, if you could call Swane normal, whose powers did seem shockingly like the magic in their texts.

Francis and Elder Farragut approached Brandon. Farragut was a man in his fifties whose arm had been replaced with a metal prosthetic that hung out of his monk-like robes. He's the one that spoke to Brandon.

"We've deemed your knowledge adequate for joining the order as an acolyte. To be a full member you'll be joining Francis in his quest to find a new piece of ancient technology. The two of you will be leaving in the morning." He turned and walked off without awaiting a reply.

"I have a pair of robes for you." Francis smiled.

Bells rang at the front gates. The two of them ran to see what was going on. Four scouts wearing tanned hide armor with sheathed bows were coming in and a small crowd gathered around them. One of them walked with the aid of another - a crude bandage wrapped around his right leg.

"We found it! We found it!" the leader of their group continued exclaiming.

"Share what you idiots are blathering about!" Swane said, happily, as he approached.

"We found it! The Dragon's lair! We found it!" the scout replied.

* * *

Gertrude and the girl sat down in an abandoned gas station eating pieces of pemmican they had traded hog meat for in Delta on the old highway going north. They were almost done with the ninety-mile hike to Waco.

"Thanks." Gwen said.

Gerti looked at her confused.

"For sticking around and looking for me." Gwen explained.

"Don't worry about it." Gerti said, while suppressing a grin.

A couple days later they were approaching the ironwork bridge that crossed over the Brazos River and directly into the heart of what had become of Waco.

A concrete wall rose up ten feet on the other side of the bridge. Even from here they could both see the guards walking the wall.

The market was in full swing in an old parking lot that surrounded a large circular building. The guards called down to them to wait while they opened the gate. They immediately identified Gerti by her attire. The guards asked for the rifles, Gwen was hesitant but obeyed when she saw Gerti surrendering hers.

They walked through the parking lot market until they came upon a shop selling vegetables out of a wheelbarrow shaded by a sheet metal awning. An older man stood behind it and smiled when he looked up and saw them approaching.

"Mr. Gropht." Gerti said with a smile.

He came around the wheelbarrow and hugged her tight.

"I didn't think I was going to see you again," he said. Mr. Gropht had always been an avuncular, if not also troublesome, figure for the children growing up in Waco. He had sold a pistol to Gerti when she was thirteen - a highly illegal thing to have in the walls.

After introductions were made there, Gerti took the girl to her dad's clinic a little ways away in the old student housing. They walked through a neighborhood of new construction houses made of concrete debris and clay-mud mortar.

Small crowds milled around the town going about their business. When they arrived, her dad's assistant was the only one in the clinic at that moment. Beth Ellington was a girl a bit older than Gerti. She always seemed like she knew the punchline to an unsaid joke and that always bothered Gerti but she was a good hand around the clinic.

"Welcome back Gertrude, I see you made a friend out there," she said, with a slight smile.

Gerti ignored Beth's expression.

"Thank you Beth. This is Gwen. Do you know where my folks are?" Gerti asked.

"Your dad's visiting Arthur Collins and your mom is out hunting. She should be back in a few days."

"I'm going to see the council. Gwen's gonna hang out here until I come back." Gerti said.

"Wait, what?" Gwen asked.

"The council'll want to see me alone. Sorry." Gerti said.

Gwen agreed.

Gerti left and made a bee-line through the inner wall to the council's chambers in the university. Once she walked through the inner wall the crowd changed from ratty shod wastelanders to robed men and women with holier than thou looks on their faces. Clean shaven men - jewelry clad women.

She found the auditorium where she had been given her task originally. Large doors and two guards armed with ornate spears blocked her path into the room. She explained why she was there and one escorted her into the room after patting her down for weapons.

Twelve figures robed in dark green sitting around a large table abruptly stopped their discussion when she and the guard walked in.

"Gertrude Alvarez," one of them said in a gruff and disdainful voice.

"Yessir."

"Were you able to accomplish your project?"

She pulled the flash drive out of a pocket and held it up for them to see.

The council erupted. Some were jubilant while others were furious and yelling at their colleagues. One of the council members who had been celebrating quickly motioned to the guard to remove Gerti, then followed them out of the door.

"Estrevor, lead us to the Ferrell. Enfilade, get the researchers and bring them to Ferrell as well. Tell them Gertrude's back," he commanded.

He was an old man but whatever was going on made him move like he suddenly remembered being young. A gleam in his eye made Gerti nervous. Enfilade took off at a run while Estrevor led them out towards the parking lot market that surrounded the domed building. Gerti could still hear yelling from inside the council chambers. She had never heard of the council being anything but a monolithic, single faced, entity that moved in unison.

"What's going on?" she asked

"Don't ask questions, Girl. Just be glad you're here to see a new era," the council member responded.

They approached the Ferrell building. There were four council guards standing outside the only unblocked doors going into the building. Nobody from the outer circle had ever been allowed in this building. Gerti always assumed it was a food cache or something else mundane. That thought seemed unlikely to her now.

The guards moved out of the way and Estrevor led them into a box room overlooking a dark and vast opening in front of them.

Gerti couldn't see anything through the window.

A few minutes passed and Enfilade entered the room preceding four people wearing glasses and the white robes of the higher level researchers. They were all beside themselves with excitement.

One of them, a man with black hair and the stubble of someone who's forgotten to shave for several days, approached Gerti and held out his hand. She handed him the flash drive. He plugged it into a computer and began navigating the interfaces. A progress bar filled and he sat back satisfied.

"Gertrude, you have no idea how big of a deal this is," the researcher said with a smile. "Will someone get the lights on - we'll need to check the state of -"

Getrude stopped listening as the lights came on and she saw the room below.

An old arena surrounded in rows of seating. In the middle of the arena were rows and rows of pristine Trustee bots coming to life and unlimbering after a hundred years of dormancy.

In the midst of the Trustee Bots was a single larger model robot that Gerti didn't recognize. It was the size of a small building - made of angular metal plates. Running lights flickered to life along its surface as it began to hover a few feet off the ground. Gerti saw what looked like plasma gun barrels electrifying all over its body.

"I'd like to see the traitors fight these," the council member said, chuckling to himself.

'Oh God, what have I done?'

Find out what happens next in:
SCORCHED EARTH: VOLUME II

Available now in print and eBook formats on Amazon

and StoryboundPublishing.com

If you enjoyed this book, please consider leaving

us a glowing review! Thank you!

ETHAN MOORE has wanted to be a writer for as long as he can remember, but it wasn't until his brother-in-law introduced him to the world of tabletop roleplaying that his creative spark found a home. One summer, a single campaign with his brother-in-law and a friend ignited what would become years of immersive storytelling and worldbuilding.

For the next eight years, Ethan took on the mantle of "forever DM" for his friend group, crafting intricate campaigns filled with settings, characters, and lore based off that first game. His curiosity pulled him deep into research, exploring everything from religion and politics to history, law, blacksmithing, meteorology, programming, and beyond - interests that naturally wove themselves into his storytelling. As a homeschooled student, this self-guided mode of learning felt not just natural, but essential.

When the game sessions began to fade - friends moving away, schedules filling up - the idea of preserving their adventures in novel form took hold. Now, Ethan writes to share the worlds and characters born from years of collaboration and imagination, hoping others will find the same wonder his friends once did around the table.

* 9 7 8 1 9 6 8 6 1 2 1 2 2 *